#FutureProof

Chris Malone

Content compiled for publication by
Richard *Mayers of Burton Mayers Books.*
First published by Burton Mayers Books 2023.

A CIP catalogue record for this book is available from the British Library
ISBN: 9781739367527
Typeset in **Garamond**

www.BurtonMayersBooks.com

DEDICATION

#FutureProof is dedicated to the one and only original *Tomb Team*; Charlotte, Heather, Ken, me and Yvor, and our two legendary cats. We had songs, a head consultant, operators, refreshment consultants, jumps consultants, saving consultants, and we were the best in the world. Shave now!

CONTENTS

ACKNOWLEDGMENTS

I am grateful to my publisher, Richard Mayers, not only for his support with #FutureProof, but with #stoptheglitch and #isolate as well. Thank you, also, to my husband, Ken, critical friend, & provider of endless cups of tea (cars tea).

1: CAERNEF

Caernef is the only home I have known. It has been a strange upbringing, immersed in a counter-culture, roaming the headlands alone, collecting specimens. I have been sheltered from the realities of the streets, out on our remote headland, and yet hooked-into the espionage that has always surrounded Miranda and Robin, the invincible puppet-masters. Chalk and cheese. Robin, venerable and wise, with insights that astound us all, and Miranda, who sweeps you up in a veil of intrigue and never quite allows you to see the goodness in it. Robin trusts. Robin listens, reassures and cares with a passion that seems to intensify as she grows increasingly frail. But Miranda is wicked. Just downright wicked.

My parents want the best for me, but they simply don't understand. They tell me, on a daily basis, to ignore Miranda, not to become caught up in her world. But I watch them watching me, as I am pulled magnetically into Miranda's aura. She's a survivor, sharp, and fleet of foot. She always beats me in the water and over rough terrain, but tells me *not for long*. She jokes that, when she and Robin retire gracefully, I am next in line, so I must train hard. It's not a joke to me. It's deadly serious, but I don't fit her stereotype. I try, but I'm not built for it.

Mum and Dad want me to stay at home, and focus on my studies, on the camp, and on building a respectable future, like Cai, the model brother, who does everything right. But I see the sadness in their eyes, as with trepidation, they try to understand my passion for *her* ways. They tell me to sit with *Robin*, out on the rocks overlooking the estuary, because she holds the wisdom we all seek. But I am desperate to earn one of Miranda's rare smiles, when she eventually turns up, which isn't often these days.

My friends from school are content living in virtuality most of the time. They don't understand why I take such a strong stand against it, but Robin's words rattle in my head, *human beings were not made to exist through their fingertips, attached to artificial devices. Put it away Poppy. Put it away.*

So, I sacrificed the gameplay. I sacrificed the reward stakes and the virtual friends. The trouble is that when you see it all from the outside, the sham complicity is so obvious. Where others exist in their created worlds as perfect human beings, sculpted using hi-tech apps and the most expensive character-building software, I remain rough and ready. Short and plump, with real mud on my shoes and wind in my hair. I know I will never be a superhero like Miranda and so I worry, secretly.

Nathan Price has made his zillions on the back of people's desire to be different. Their quest for the perfect identity fulfilled. Genius rewarded, Miranda says. But I remember the day of the great split, and it wasn't pretty. He was always kind to me, Nathan. He used to give me his prototypes to play with and listened to my ideas for new gadgets and gizmos. Arcadian B was the best of all, back in the early days, when I wasn't tall enough to reach his designing bench, and had to stand on a wooden box. I remember him handing me the beautiful silver bee, saying he had received it from China, but it wasn't activated. However, I realised my Arcadian B had powers.

The great split came soon after I used his silver gizmo to help Miranda, who was courageously rescuing Robin from capture. That was the beginning of my lifelong bond with Miranda. It was the day before I witnessed Robin throw Nathan out, forever.

I was playing quietly behind the herb beds at Caernef, small for a six-year-old, and dwarfed by the culinary jungle. As it was deep summer, the foliage was high and fragrant: deep bushed fennel and dry wispy quaking grass, which rattled if you brushed past. I was totally hidden from view. It was a chance meeting, as Robin and Miranda were walking back down towards the folly after breakfast, and Nathan was hurtling across the field carrying a bundle of wires and antennae. He tripped, metal objects went flying into the scrubby grass, he swore, and scrabbled around picking the bits up.

It was then that Robin fired him. Told him to go from Caernef forever. I was shocked.

As the distraught figures disappeared over the field, I ran home to tell Cai what I had heard.

That was ten years ago, and ironically it was the making of Nathan. He stayed for a while, but eventually set up independently and registered all his new software under the *virtuality* brand. Miranda says good on him for taking the opportunity. Now he's a zillionaire and owns the biggest virtual reality platform on the planet. He even offered me a role in his character-design studio in the school holidays, but I declined, politely. That's not where my interests lie.

....

I am only concerned with nature. Restoring, rescuing and championing. Nature. It's out of fashion, but that strengthens my resolve. After the pandemics, when I was young, people turned to nature for solace, but they soon forgot how much they needed the reassurance of open spaces. The satisfaction they gained from exercising in wild places became a distant memory. The stimulation of roughing it outdoors was superseded by simulation; an infatuation with screen comfort. Virtuality took over. A decade of decadence conveniently labelled recovery, but mainstreaming.

The worst thing about virtuality is that it appears to be free of charge. Kids are sucked in at an early age. Then, as they climb the ladders of illusory success, the fees are slipped in. Proud parents cough up. Teenagers earn points to fund their habit, consequently a lifetime commitment to the ubiquitous platform is secured. It is consuming the human race across the planet.

They would rather explore *real* places from the comfort of their sofa, to *be* the people they aren't. Apologists say *virtuality* has solved the mental health crisis, but I am not convinced.

Some days I feel like a lone voice, lost in a wilderness of realities. The outdated eco-warrior. Other days, when I link up with like-minded Caernef rebels, I am able to focus on the one and only purpose of my life, to rescue the earth from the slough of blinkered self-seeking game-players. To rescue minibeasts, grasshoppers, ladybirds and ants. To rescue the curlew in the estuary, the sparrow in the street. I don't care about the people. They are only causing irrevocable damage, what's more, I don't care about their virtual pets.

Of course, I can't save the planet by endlessly walking the cliffs of Caernef, the Welsh backwater where I grew up. That is why I need Miranda. She has friends in high places. She is tapped into the heart of government, and she goes to the conferences, making the speeches.

Robin simply agrees with me. But she has given up, retreating to her folly, the magical clifftop tower, where she reads, writes a little, and watches the estuary. She feeds off her memories of insurgence, endlessly recalling the days when she was the inspiration for the earths, the runners, the rebels who surrounded me throughout my younger days. But once Nathan jumped ship, once virtuality caught hold, Robin retreated into herself. Then the runners became the victim of their own success, adopted by the state to hold together a largely home-based virtual society. The runners became mainstream. They lost the rebellious edge that I remember so well from my early childhood. Nowadays, Robin is fragile.

As a consequence of all this, I am standing on a platform at Oxford train station, gripping a brown paper parcel, and heading back to Caernef. Oblivious members of the public, no more than a dozen, stand waiting for the train. They represent the virtuality-dependent generation; adventure addicts who fail to notice the bedraggled wagtail seeking crumbs between the benches. They are each ninety-nine per cent in someone else's imagination, and one per cent aware of the enormous hydrogen train sailing noiselessly into the platform. They somehow avoid each other as they enter the carriage. There are no steps, so their continuous experience remains uninterrupted. They ignore me; the only free spirit boarding the Alstom.

So, I did succeed in meeting with Miranda earlier today, which is an achievement in itself, due to her busy schedule. Instead of Robin's revolutionary army, a new class of people is emerging. They sail confidently above the virtuality-addicted masses. Miranda is one of these *controllers*; those who have secured influence through their connections, and who spurn virtuality, favouring what they refer to as *hard-won affluence*. Robin is disparaging about Miranda. So are my parents. But I know the game my heroine is playing, hopping on board whatever power trip the new elite is offering, obeying their rules with disguised scorn. Only … I see the look in Miranda's eye betraying her innermost thoughts. She is after one thing and one thing only; securing *her* vision for #FutureProof. But it is clear to me that Miranda is not entirely invincible.

I plant myself across the aisle from a middle-aged man dressed as his favourite virtuality avatar, complete with helmet, cape and boots. But no weapon, just a game controller. Twenty-first century irony: swords into digital ploughshares, and the illusion of control. He doesn't, of course, notice me.

Out of the window, a heron fishes in the canal,

unaware of our majestically quiet ecotrain. The Alstom has been perfected: zero carbon with the added bonus of a smooth ride so you are hardly aware you are travelling. It is good to be heading home to Caernef.

While I believe Miranda's #FutureProof to be a top-down elitist survival plot, Robin's faltering #FutureProof is a genuine attempt to save the planet from the grassroots up. I straddle the two. Intent on somehow restoring, even enhancing, the natural world, I can see Miranda's wisdom in harnessing corporate and governmental powers to focus on survival.

But.

But …

Miranda's vision comes at a cost that I dare not think about too deeply, and that I do not yet fully understand.

…………

Earlier today, Miranda was supreme, as ever. Her minions scurried around attending to her projects, her terse communications driving forward her perverse whims. As I entered, she was sitting in the controller's chair.

'Poppy, how lovely to see you after such a long time. Come here. Sit down. Coffee? Tea?'

A timid member of Miranda's staff interrupted, passing a digital dossier to her, while throwing a wary smile at me.

For a few minutes I was subservient to the dossier. Then she snapped into action, forgetting the drinks, ushering me closer where we could speak in relative privacy.

'I have something for Robin that must be delivered by hand. You understand?'

Master of the rhetorical question.

'Yes Miranda, but …'

'No, that's fine Poppy. You must carry it safely to Robin as soon as you are back at Caernef …'

As she mentions Caernef, her strident voice softens. The fact that it still plays on her heart strings doesn't escape me, despite her attempt at the bluster of a cover-up, flicking her hair, inventing a smile.

'Caernef Miranda?'

'Yes. I need you to transfer it to Robin, and let me know it has been done. It's nothing much, more sentimental than anything, but Robin adores you. She'll take it from you Poppy, I know it.' Miranda's head is full with her schemes, which is why I travelled all the way to see her.

I am only just five foot tall, and as Miranda rose from the chair, I felt like a child again. She uses her height to her advantage. A benefit I will never have, unless, as my brother Cai points out regularly, I enter virtuality. I would be able to create an avatar as tall as the young aspen on the bank of the streams behind Caernef.

Mustering all my courage, I began, 'Miranda, I want you to tell me more about #FutureProof.'

'Why?'

I knew I must respond quickly otherwise her brain would have moved on, and I would have missed my chance. I looked her in the eye, 'If I am to represent the next generation. If I am to succeed you and Robin, I *need* to know.'

'Need to know. Hm. Okay. There will be an important role for you to play in #FutureProof; you do need to understand.'

But she paused, due to a digital alarm sounding in her pocket, retrieved a device, checked the screen, then left, without a word. I stood beside her massive black chair, dangling vacant from a hook in the ceiling; the latest fad, and I waited. Oh Miranda; I am not your priority, but you want to get something to Robin, so, today, you need me.

I lingered; loosely confident she would return.

Left alone in Miranda's opulent office, I was rooted to the spot, aware I should be capitalising on the opportunity, but too nervous of security cameras. I cast my gaze nonchalantly across her desk. Tickets for international travel to Syria, my parents' original home, to Italy, to

North Korea. North Korea? #FutureProof emblazoned on letterheads, on the equipment, except for the package I am holding now. Brown paper old-style. A gift for Robin.

She had forgotten to lock her screen. A spreadsheet was open. Across the room my eyes could just about read the list of countries signed up to her #FutureProof. Many green ticks, including China and Russia. Just as I was reading the red list: North Korea, Libya, Somalia, Miranda returned. Dior Poison, her signature smell. Fresh lipstick. Were there more rebel countries beyond the edge of the screen, or were there only three left to persuade? To persuade to do what exactly?

'Sorry Poppy; good of you to come all this way to collect my parcel for Robin. Was there anything else?'

Feeling brave, I asserted myself, 'I only just heard about your parcel. I'm here to ask you about #FutureProof, remember?'

'Of course.' She looked over my head towards someone signalling to her through the internal window.

'And?' I repressed my frustration.

'Of course. Now, #FutureProof means different things to different people.'

'I know that,' I prompted, an enforced patience hanging in the air between us.

'#FutureProof means the redemption of the planet. It is the saving of mankind …'

'And nature?'

'What? Nature? But of course.'

'Miranda, you say I have an important part to play. What is my part? Tell me what I must do.'

Miranda stooped down towards me, looking beneficent, benevolent, even, maybe, kind, 'My dear Poppy. Don't you worry about it. There will be a very important part for you to perform. Perhaps two parts; you and your double, but I have so much to organise first. I need more partners on board. Best thing you can do is complete your studies, keep out of trouble, stay below the radar. We will call for you. You need to grow up a bit first. Not yet.'

'Not yet.'

'No, but if you can take this to Robin, even persuade her to join in with my #FutureProof, I would be grateful.' Miranda handed me the parcel, which I examined with interest. It was tied with some of Nathan's heavily marketed digital string, only to be broken by the designated recipient. She grabbed a pen and scrawled 'Robin FitzWilliam, Caernef, by hand,' on the top right-hand corner, but as she was handing it to me, she had second thoughts, pulled it back, rested it on her knee and wrote something else, patted me on the head and ushered me on my way.

It is definitely worthwhile to be travelling four hundred miles to Oxford and back for a few grains of gold dust from Miranda. Firstly, I am pleased to be asserting my independence. Secondly, I have reminded her I exist. I now know she will not forget me so easily, especially if I prove myself useful. I wonder what is in the parcel and why she doesn't send it with a courier. I wrangle with the desire to delicately slide off the digital string, to open it, but resist. It is for Robin, not for me. If I was being Miranda, I would of course sneak a look, but I am growing out of the desire to actually *be* her. I need to be Poppy. Honest. Boring. The old-fashioned eco-warrior who spurns virtuality.

I read her scrawled afterthought: *Persons with any weight of character carry, like planets, their atmospheres along with them in their orbits.*

Like her, of course.

....

The hydro-train lulls its occupants into their stupor of virtuality, but my brain is racing. Why is it that I adore Miranda, yet see through her? She definitely projects an aura of supreme confidence, which I admire, because I don't have it. She is still so athletic, perfectly formed for speed. Just a whiff of Dior Poison and my heart races.

However, one scene from my earliest years, plays and replays in my mind. It haunts my dreams, troubling my waking hours. I have never broached it with my parents, but I am sure. Really sure.

My first recollection is of two menacing thugs coming into our home, the cottage on the Caernef clifftop, when I was very young. Mum and Robin were with me and they were scared. The men had guns. Weirdly, I can remember being asked to read my storybook to them. I think they were trying to gain my trust, but I hated them, instinctively. With cruel eyes above their masks, their honeyed words were tainted with hypocrisy. At that young age I knew, intuitively, not to trust them. They showed me some old photographs, demanding answers, but Mum protected me, and they left. I must have gone to bed, but I couldn't sleep for ages. I heard Dad with his friend Gid, coming back from The Prince of Wales. Only then did I sleep. Odd things have always happened at Caernef, but that was one of the worst for me, an innocent four-year-old. I was left secretly harbouring a sinking suspicion. Home felt slightly unsafe.

And that is not the most disturbing memory. After the incident of the masked men, I can recall Mum, again, protecting me. She huddled me into her skirt. I saw the mud on her boots, felt the rasp of the fabric on my cheeks, and smelled the woodsmoke. Peering out, despite Mum's attempts to shield me, with hindsight, I am certain I saw Miranda. It was most definitely Miranda; except she was the enemy. Dressed all in black, with the harsh face of an adversary. She was threatening the Caernef people, my family and my close friends. Mum carried me off, running to the shed where the vegetables were stored over winter, escaping before Miranda and the men in black saw us. Mum comforted me as we crouched behind the sacks of potatoes and carrots, chilled to the bone. Then I remember we ran through the darkness to the folly, where we were safe. Robin's folly has always felt like a refuge.

Despite my adoration of her, I have never completely trusted Miranda as a result of this bizarre memory.

....

The Alstom draws into Birmingham, and I change trains, unsettled by recalling these strangely dark early memories. I don't forget Robin's parcel, and grip it tightly as I scuttle between platforms, holding my nose as I pass the fast-food joints. Down-at heel vendors, beggars and massive adverts for Nathan's virtuality.

....

As soon as I am back at Caernef, I head for Robin.

Catching my breath, I top the rise above the parade ground, remembering what is so special about my home. Greeted by the call of a cormorant, fishing in the far distance, I grin to myself and rush towards the folly. I am carrying out a mission for Miranda. An important mission. Robin is on the step waiting for me. She has to hold the door frame to steady herself in the gusting sea-wind. Her fibromyalgia is bad at the moment, moreover she struggles to see or hear clearly, so she doesn't notice me until I am close by.

'Poppy, it is so good to see you back. Safe at Caernef again. Your Mum will be relieved. We don't like you spending time away with *her*. Come on in and tell me all about it.'

I just smile. Caernef is Robin, and Robin is Caernef. Although, as she often reminds me, I was here before her, as a sweet toddler. Mum and Dad camped out, illegally, in the cottage, when Caernef was originally up for sale. That was before Robin bought the camp, making it into the success it is today. It is one of those legendary stories often told sitting by the fire on a cold, dark winter's evening.

As if reading my thoughts, Robin reflects, 'Sometimes, Poppy, I catch a glimpse of your cheerful face, and I think you haven't changed at all since those early days when you scampered down here to show me your treasures.'

'And other times Robin?'

'Other times I worry that you are only just beginning to hold your own in a world that has become too hazardous … too rotten at the core … it's not a good time to be growing up. I worry for you.'

In an attempt to ease her anxiety, I produce the Miranda's package from behind my back, with its digital string still intact. 'Shall I read the inscription for you?' I ask keenly, aware she is squinting at Miranda's scrawl on the front of the brown package.

'Yes. Yes, please Poppy.'

I have already read it a hundred times; it sounds so like Miranda herself, 'Persons with any weight of character carry, like planets, their atmospheres along with them in their orbits.'

'Ah.'

'What does it mean Robin? Is it code?'

'I don't think so. It refers to Mrs Yeobright. But it does tell me what is inside the parcel, and I don't really want those troubles again.'

Disappointed, I wait for her to open it, but she plucks the string, twanging it like a musical beat, before ripping it off, then handing the package back to me, saying, 'You have it, Poppy. Keep it safe because it records all sorts of shenanigans from the last decade. Things that remain outside the realm of digital evidence. Might be needed one day to let our slippery heroine Miranda off the hook.' She winds the digital string neatly round her finger, ties it off, and slips it into the tiny kitchen drawer. Just string, as the spell is broken. It will probably end up as a plant tie.

'Are you sure?'

'Yes, I am sure. I'm well out of their games now.'

'Miranda said you should join in her #FutureProof?'

'Rubbish. No way. #FutureProof means one thing and one thing only: getting this planet back on to the straight and narrow. Listening to nature. Eschewing the ridiculous fripperies that mankind has created.'

'Eschewing?'

She laughs, wearily, but for an instant, her old twinkle returns. 'It means giving up.'

I brew some tea, and we relocate upstairs in Robin's lookout, where she is most comfortable. I sit on her bunk while she sits on her handmade rainbow cushion, which graces the one small wooden chair. We both stare out into the estuary. While I gulp my large mug of tea, she sips at her small tea cup. She has become an old lady ahead of her time, over the last few years.

'Tell me, Poppy, what exactly did Miranda tell you about her version of #FutureProof?'

'She didn't really tell me anything. It was most frustrating.'

I don't elicit more out of Robin as she slips into one of her deep reveries. Eventually, I rise, saying I will drop in to see her again soon. As I am about to descend the narrow staircase, she holds her hands out to receive Miranda's parcel from me, gently whispering, 'Thank you. Maybe I'd better check this out after all.'

2: THE ARCADE

'Poppy come here and pay attention.'

'What?'

'Don't you *what* me.'

'Sorry Dad. What do you want?' I force a smile.

'Where were you last night?' You had only just returned from Oxford. From seeing *Her Majesty*. Your mother was worried. I was worried. All you had to do was message us.'

Misplaced suspicion. They are unwilling to let me go, but they don't know what to challenge. Dad is sound. He and Mum care. I grit my teeth, presenting the innocent face of the dutiful daughter. 'After I visited Robin, I went to the arcade. As usual.'

'You weren't there at nine. I messaged you.'

'I was.'

'You weren't. Home by ten. Every night. You agreed, even if you have been cavorting with your idol in Oxford. That ...'

'I was home by ten.'

An uncomfortable stalemate.

'Anyway, have you sent in your options submission yet? We keep asking you.'

'Not yet. I'm thinking about it.'

'You've had plenty of time to think about it. Did you ask Robin for *her* advice? You know the *right* choice. Just opt for the four sciences. You can do it standing on your head, especially the environmental modules. You have covered most of the syllabus already.'

'Hmmm.' Mum and Dad are passionate scientists through and through.

I walk off before he can explode with *Don't you Hmmm me.* I want to study the arts. I want to tackle new ground. I'm bored with the ecological arguments, the evidence, the modelling. Gloom and doom. I'm depressed by it all. But if I could immerse myself in contemporary and classical art, music, poetry and drama, I would be happy. Making *my* choices, not those expected of me. Trouble is, I need a parental signature, unless I continue to stall. Once I am sixteen on September the first, I can complete the application as an independent student. I could even opt for complete online learning, with no pressure to face the artificially sculpted characters of fellow students, lining Nathan's pockets with their virtuality subscriptions.

I know what Robin would say, *Follow your heart, Poppy. What do you really want; what will inspire you, fulfil you, ultimately improving the world for others? You must future-proof your existence as well as that of the planet* … Miranda, if she took the time to think about me, would toss her head in scorn telling me to stand up for … stand up for what? She would say, *Cut the crap Poppy; play the system* …

…………

Before he left, when I was only six years old, I let Nathan experiment on me. He said it would come in useful one day, if it worked. He wasn't sure. Generally, I forget about it, but every so often my arm aches where he injected the tiny geotracker deep into the flesh. It bled, and was sore for a while, but I treated it with disinfectant wipes like he showed me, so it healed over pretty quickly. Hidden. It is under the top of my left arm, in the muscle, and it is meant to protect me throughout my life. If I am ever in trouble, I can activate it by following a crude sequence of slaps on my arm, apparently unable to be accidentally replicated, but I'm not so sure. We hid it from Mum and Dad. I ignore it most of the time, until it flutters under the skin, letting me know it is still there. I've never used it. I wonder if its power runs out over time. It still flutters now and then, even after ten years. On reflection, in his naivety, he took advantage of an innocent child, but in those early days of experimental virtuality-type tech, Nathan and I were co-conspirators. It just seemed exciting.

Later, Nathan perfected the implants, linking them to his virtuality platform, so before long, they replaced piercings as the vogue. He also added security features.

These days Nathan's geo-trackers protect personal avatars out on the virtual streets. They are a big earner for virtuality, and now offer heavy protection for gamers, with safeguarding software alongside minimum-age restrictions. Most parents buy them for the reassurance, after some unfortunate high-profile cases of digital abuse.

Generally, virtuality is not questioned. It is *the* way of life for everyday people, of all ages.

Take Autumn, a boy at school, one of the nicer ones. He spends hours each day, after lessons, plugged into the sports package. Nathan boasts that you can *be* anyone. Inhabit the skin of your heroes. Autumn runs marathons, trains with top flight footballers, and swims the Channel. Then he brags online the next morning, posting screenshots, his muscles bulging below his virtual dreadlocks. Autumn is more of an artistic creation than a real boy. When he tips up at school, pale and thin, all I can think about is Nathan's worldwide deception.

Maybe one day, they will create a museum to Nathan in the arcade. After all, Caernef is the place where it all began, during the excitement of Robin's early success, even though the camp has drifted into being a nowhere at the moment. Tourists will file virtually through Nathan's old workshop, saved the inconvenience of actual travel out to the back of beyond.

I named it *the arcade* years ago, because, at the time, I was reading a story about a rebel gang hanging out in a retro seaside amusements arcade. It seemed so alluring; so different from my home environment.

There is a secret lurking deep inside the place. I have told no one. It feels inevitable that one day I will end up telling Miranda. Cai has just about guessed, so I will have to come clean with him, or lie, Miranda-style, but lying doesn't feel right. It's a dilemma.

Nathan set up the platform in the arcade months before he left, but he never finished the project. I used to follow him, at a distance. Then one evening, at dusk, when he left the workshop to return for supper in the camp, I was brave. I crept down the path, and found the digital key, which I had watched him hide under a flowerpot; Caernef's bizarre old-style tech sitting comfortably with cutting-edge innovations. By the light of my phone, I stole past his stacked cyber-junk. Passing dead screens, the debris of failed projects alongside work-in-progress, I was drawn to a distant glow, and was not disappointed when I reached the back of the shed. He had created a circular area, a metre across, under the sloping ceiling so even I had to stoop. Set in the far wall, sitting on a slab of rock, was the centrepiece of his latest scheme. A cross between something from the Tardis and spare parts from a satellite. Ever since I took over the arcade, I have covered it with an oilcloth, so the iridescent glow isn't visible.

Nathan, like me, loved the wildlife out at Caernef. Many of his cybergames replicate the birds and creatures, raising them to mythical heights while investing them with new powers. Arcadian B was the best ever. This glowing phenomenon had started as an Arcadian B, and I knew what that could achieve. Nathan had encased the silver body of the bee in an iridescent gossamer thread, like a spider's nest in the early morning.

There was no evidence of a power source. I was young and didn't understand, but it fascinated me. That was the beginning of my regular secret visits to the arcade, pretending I was Miranda. For a while Nathan was my hero, until Robin sent him packing, when his workshop was avoided like a bad smell. He left in such a hump that he didn't tidy up or retrieve anything. I hid my excitement as I watched him depart never to return, claiming the arcade for my own, concealing the glowing platform under the heavy cloth.

Caernef is a strange place. Unlike Robin, I am not in love with the wild headland, and I do not over-romanticise the camp she rescued so many years ago, now an eco-community hosting expensive off-grid experiences as well as the school visits, which were originally its bread and butter. Although even that has been outsourced. I grew up with the freedom to roam within the perimeter fences. Caernef is home, but it is not my nirvana, and I am keen to break out of the wild yet homely square mile. I ache to leave it all behind: the hum of our turbines on a windy night, the allotments, the chickens, the solar arrays, the microgrid and the camp fires. I yearn for Miranda's lifestyle, in a wider world of risk, excitement and romance.

Robin let me take over the arcade. She is kind. Once Nathan had gone, tail between his legs, she caught me in there, sifting through the debris. I was looking for the activator, a compact remote switch that I had seen Nathan use to operate the Arcadian platform. I feared he had taken it when he left. Hearing someone approaching, I knew it was too late to hide, so stood my ground.

Robin pushed the door wide open, glaring inside the arcade, but when she saw me, she relaxed, 'Oh, it's only you Poppy. That's alright then. My goodness what a mess in here.'

'Would you like me to tidy up?'

'That would be really helpful. Thank you. I don't want to see any of this disgusting cyber-junk again. Can you get someone to help you take the rubbish up to the gorge, so we can bury it?'

The dusty arcade of Nathan's discarded rubbish became my playground, as they left the shed alone for me and my childish imaginings.

'You spend far too much time down in that old shed,' Mum nagged.

But they never stopped me, and they were always too busy to trek the half-mile down the path to check what I was doing. The arcade started to define my reality. The cottage, which has been my only real home, is too small for a growing family, but Mum and Dad won't move. I don't think they can afford to. Putting that aside, they love the place, having created somewhere special, invested with their history. The cottage was their refuge when they were on the run, homeless with me only a toddler. Robin rescued them, and they made the cottage their home, working in the outdoor centre. It holds many good memories for me, as well as the dark moments. The tiny lounge is often packed with our friends from the camp, and sometimes strange maverick visitors, the fire is lit in winter, and the old rusty windows are thrown wide to the air of the clifftop in summer. We can, of course, use the dormitories, when the camp is closed. Cai and I enjoyed many a sleepover with our friends as young children, but that was before *virtuality*.

So, I gradually shifted my books, my school things, and my collections, down into the arcade.

'You will be sleeping down there next,' Mum chided, knowing, but not admitting, that I was growing too old to share the cramped bedroom with Cai and all his virtuality paraphernalia.

....

For as long as I can remember, after school, when the evenings are lighter, I have collected finds from the fields and woods of Caernef. I sort them into three categories: specimens I will give away as presents, items to use in my art, as well as a few pure keepers. If I move away from Caernef, the keepers will fit into a box. They are part of me now, telling the tale of my life, from the exquisite tiny white cowrie shell I found nestled between stones down by the estuary when I was only just starting my collection, to the original oak apple Nathan used when he created his first ecotech device, the oke. Only I know it is the *actual* oak apple Nathan studied. I watched him turn it over and over, replicating it in wood, burying the transponder inside. Due to Nathan's celebrity status, it is probably worth thousands now. But that doesn't interest me.

There are butterfly wings, crispy grasshopper skeletons, crab's claws, even a shark's tooth. I have curious pebbles, rattling seed pods and feathers. My favourite is the brittle adder skin I found under a rock near the cliff edge. I have occasionally seen adders. The skin was an early find.

But I'm struggling to see a future for me, with a cardboard box of natural curiosities, in a world characterised by exponential tech. That's why I played at being Miranda, to give myself her survivability, her cutting edge. I know I need to be more like Miranda to succeed out there. Robin's ideals are all very well. She spouts worthy philosophy and still has swathes of followers, believing in the simple alternative to the tech, but it is so old school. It is naïve. No one under the age of fifty really believes in it any more.

....

'If you are going to continue your campaigns you will need the most up to date science at your fingertips.' Mum is in persuasive mode.

'I want to create. To look ahead, not backwards.'

'So, science is backward-thinking, is it?'

'I didn't mean that … I … just don't believe people are listening to science these days.'

'Rubbish. Where did you get that idea from?'

'From looking around me.'

'At Caernef? I don't think so. It will be Miranda, miss high-and-mighty, who has planted such thoughts in your mind, no doubt.'

Dad joins the attack, 'If you don't seize the opportunity right now Poppy, it will be too late. You can see the consequences already. The sky is darker, the pollution is thicker even out here. You know first-hand how species are being decimated, how this ridiculous obsession with virtuality is skewing the focus of the younger generation …'

'Dad, I know. I know. Can't you see; I know all this. I just …'

'Yes? We're listening. You just …' A heavy silence falls into our nervous triangle, rendering my brain numb.

I try, 'It's just that …' Heaven knows why I can't talk to people any more. It all makes sense up in my head. I try again, 'It's just that I see people ignoring the rational arguments. I see them at school, and on Cai's screens. I listen to them talk about virtuality. I think of Nathan, and I feel sort of responsible. The only way to persuade the younger generation to understand how precarious things are at the moment is to talk *their* language.'

My parents are listening. Actually listening. They pause, nodding in agreement. Mum launches the retaliation, 'So Poppy, talk their language from an informed position. Be ahead of the climate game. Understand everything there is to know. Predict. Project. Show them, through their platforms. Show them. That's what Robin would say to you, I am convinced.'

Dad however, is more pensive. 'What are you saying to us Poppy?' Try to explain.'

If I am to convince my parents I should study arts, now is the time, but I am struck dumb; instead, I pout. Taking her cue from my glowering face, Mum heads to the kitchen, muttering that they have enough other stuff to worry about at the moment, and puts the anachronistic kettle on the hob to boil. Just as she always has done. I am about to slink away when Dad gathers me up in his arms, like he used to. 'Don't go yet Poppy. Try again. I am listening.'

He smells of soil and onions. His rough shirt rubs my cheek primevally, like it did when I was young. I take a deep breath, 'Dad, when I study the science, I get so …'

He doesn't jump in, like Mum, to provide easy answers for me. Instead, he cuddles me, waiting patiently.

'You get so …'

'It's a mix of angry and depressed. It makes me feel bad. Responsible. Powerless. Hopeless. I don't want to feel like that, but I desperately want to make a difference. You and Mum don't understand.'

'Try me.'

I pull away from his gentle grasp, look into his eyes, and I try him. 'I want to study the arts. Real art, not digital. I want to understand more about the way music, art, words, can touch people where science has failed.' I tense with anxiety. Honesty doesn't always pay off with parents. This could blow sky high.

'I see. That makes sense to me now. I'll talk with Mum. When is the deadline for the options submission?'

'Friday.'

'This Friday?'

'Yes.' He cuffs me gently around the head, play fighting like he does with Cai, and disappears into the kitchen. I'm not going to wait. As I pad silently towards the front door, aiming for the scrubby grass of the hillside leading to the clifftop, intent on reaching the arcade where I can think, I hear Mum's raucous voice shrieking, 'She said what?' Dad hasn't a strong track record at fighting my battles with Mum. The cottage is too small. You hear everything.

Before I manage to slide out of the front door, Cai calls from upstairs, 'That you Pops?' I've been brave with Dad. To be fair, I should be brave with Cai. He can be a strong ally. I turn, shutting my ears as I hurtle past the open kitchen door and up the stairs.

Cai is taller than me already, though he is three years younger. He fills the small bedroom, which has become ninety nine percent his. My small single bed, where I crash out each night, is primarily a place where his real friends perch to play virtuality with him. I charge him rent by the hour, which he pays from his virtuality winnings. But today he is alone.

'You okay Pops?'

'Mum won't listen.'

'To what?' he focuses on the screen in front of him. I sit on *my* bed.

'To me. Cai, I want to do arts. I don't want to do sciences.' At this revelation, he turns to face me, smiling genially. Cai calms waters, makes friends, ignores difficulties. As a result, he fits seamlessly into his social world, whereas I am the wild outsider. To make sure he is listening, and not still in whatever virtual dilemma he has chosen for today's adventure, I repeat, 'I want to do arts.'

'They won't let you.'

'Then I will wait until I don't need them to.'

'Really?'

'Mmm.'

'Poppy, do arts after. That's the easiest thing. Do sciences for one year. Get the basic higher-level knowledge, then switch when it won't cause so mush upset. Mum and Dad have other things to worry about just now.'

Cai always comes up with things, and *he* hasn't spent so long listening to Robin as I have. 'Thanks. I hadn't thought of that, but I can't wait. What if things get worse? What if virtuality suddenly becomes the only way? What if the atmosphere suddenly takes another plunge in quality, what if our time on this planet is limited? The government is talking about it. I would always regret not having given the arts a chance when I had the opportunity.'

'You're determined then?'

'Yes.'

'Do you want me to put in a word with Mum and Dad?'

'Yes please Cai. Yes please.'

'I'll do what I can, but can't promise anything. Now, do you like the red or the orange background best?'

I glance despairingly at the screen, while he flips

between frames. It's a virtuality extinction platform, with sad-looking wild animals: tigers, lions with some of the manufactured cross-breeds. You have to rescue species; I know that much.

'I prefer the native wildlife, the minibeasts and smaller mammals, but for those, I would use black.'

'Black?'

'Yes. To denote extinction. With sulphurous clouds to represent mankind.'

'You sound like Robin.'

He doesn't intend to upset me. I desperately think what Miranda would say, and plump for, 'You are the game-master Cai. You choose your colour and stick to it. The red looks more like you.'

'Red it is then. Thanks.' While he turns back to the screen, I plead, 'You will remember to speak with Mum and Dad Cai?'

'I will. Don't you worry. Oh, Pops, there was a message for you from Miranda.' He leaves it dangling as bait. I freeze.

'For me? Only me, or one of those public motivational ones?'

'For you. I didn't read it. You got your phone with you?'

'No'

'Oh Poppy. Why on earth not? Okay. Hold on. We will do it dinosaur style.' He points his phone at the multifunctional, prints the message, folds it without even glancing at it, and passes it into my eager hand. I grab it, holding tight, while I run down the stairs, out of the front door, on to the path heading for the arcade.

3: TARQUIN

Miranda usually forgets about me, which is why I took the trip to see her, to plant thoughts of *me* back in her buzzing brain. She leads an important life, mixing with intriguing real-life characters. You don't need virtuality if you are Miranda. Last year she sent me a message inviting me to stay, but it caused all sorts of issues here and in the end I didn't go.

I clamber through the junk in the arcade, glancing out of the window, laced with spider's webs, just in case there is a cormorant in the estuary, and I unfold the paper. *Poppy, I need a dogsbody for a 6-week project. Summer holiday pocket money. Accom provided. Message me by Wednesday or I'll try someone else. Miranda.'*

My heart accelerates. My cheeks flush. I open the window, but the air smells rank, even out here. Can I do this? Suddenly my very ploddy life seems to be taking a new turn. So, it was definitely worth the trip to Oxford, placing myself in Miranda's eyeline, using up so much of my meagre pocket money. But my parents will *never* agree.

....

It was inevitable, and, as usual, Cai's idea. I traded a tick in the options box committing me to the four modules making up environmental science, for a summer of freedom with Miranda. Mum and Dad agreed. They're distracted. Something about the security at Caernef. Miranda has committed to chaperone me; she also promises I will get paid. There was a row, because Miranda is not trusted, but once they had agreed, they stood by their decision, although with visible reluctance.

So here I am, once again on the steps outside Oxford station, watching the ecobuses weave through the headphoned masses, marvelling at the garishness of the world beyond the safe perimeter fence of Caernef. Waiting for Miranda. Scanning, clutching the handle of my case, attempting to blend in, but feeling totally out of place. I can do this.

When she arrives, even downward-faced members of the public turn their heads. So much for being a spy, Miranda, when your very presence disturbs the equilibrium of a place. You make them stop and stare. They ignore me, but you are magnificent. Tall, dominant, decisive. Slick black running suit. Even the age-lines on your forehead have grandeur. The buses give you space, while you approach me, the overgrown kid clutching a suitcase.

'Hi, Poppy!'

'Hi, Miranda!'

'I'll explain while we drive. Due in a meeting in half an hour, so chop, chop.'

Always in a hurry. A person in demand. I run behind her across the concourse and we dive into the back of an expensive vehicle. Doors close silently. Dior Poison.

'Now, Poppy, you will stay with some friends of mine at their country club. I need you to spend your first week getting into character. Low profile. Quiet geeky kid wanting pocket money. They will give you an access pass and you will work shifts, six days a week. Some cleaning, some work in the cafeteria. Just blend in. This time next week, I will give you my instructions. Any questions?'

Totally overawed but determined not to show it, I shake my head and gaze into her bewildering eyes, trying to determine her intentions for me. We arrive at *her* destination. Throwing a scant smile in my direction, she leaves me in the car, striding purposefully into the distance. I am driven a further half mile into the outskirts. We draw up at the back entrance of a sort of conference centre. The driver opens the car door for me to step out. She says nothing, and drives off, leaving me standing on the gravel, clutching my case.

Is this a test? Am I being watched?

No one about. A stale early-summer breeze in the branches of an oak tree. It might have been a school years ago. One of the private sort, with tennis courts and prep, like in books. But it has been repainted with a corporate wash. Insignia on the sign, the door, and on a delivery van parked at the back. A black lion with flourishes.

The sign says, *Tarquin: Tradesman's Entrance*, remembering the colon and the apostrophe. I'm not a man, certainly not a tradesman, and I haven't a clue what Tarquin means, so I stand, looking helplessly at the burdock growing through cracks in the concrete, under the trees. After five minutes it seems I must do something, so I approach the Tradesman's Entrance and examine the choice of bells. One old bellpull. A newer intercom. Try the button on the intercom.

'Hello. Name?'

'Poppy.'

'Pardon?'

'Poppy.'

'Press the button when you speak.'

I press and try again, my finger taut. Embarrassed. Trying to sound confident. 'Good afternoon. My name is Poppy Kiwan.'

'Please press the button when you speak.'

I take my finger off and then try again. A loud electronic noise ensues. I jump backwards, as an impatient woman opens the door.

'Good afternoon. Miranda sent me.'

'Yes. Miranda. Come in.'

She leads me silently through narrow corridors. I smell cooking and drains before we emerge in a front-of-house entrance hall. Without looking at me, she taps a desk bell, and immediately a smart waiter appears, a bit older than me, I guess.

'Harvey, this is Poppy, Miranda's girl. Take her upstairs and run through the schedule with her.'

Harvey nods, ushering me across the polished floor, into a maze of passageways, then up some back stairs to a very untidy staffroom. He gestures to me to sit on a stained settee. Nervousness visible on my face.

'Try not to worry Poppy. I won't bite.'

I force a smile.

…………

My first week at Tarquin was so busy that I hardly remember any details. Fortunately, I am used to completing domestic tasks at speed from my stints covering voluntarily for absent domestics at Caernef Camp. Even so, I have fumbled and muddled through, not familiar with the Tarquin ways, barely assisted by Harvey or the other staff. I am clearly viewed as a timid outsider planted by Miranda. They see her as a distant, exacting patron.

No sight of Miranda, and no messages from her, which is usual. She must have a purpose in bringing me here, which I hope to discover, because she is coming to see me in five minutes time. I have been, grudgingly, awarded an early lunch break, and have been told to wait in the *vestibule*, as they call the entrance hall.

Perching on a posh chair in my pink domestic's uniform, awaiting the next step in my summer adventure. I imagine Miranda explaining to me that Tarquin is not what it seems, that there are secret rendezvous and esteemed international guests. I know what she is like, having listened into her conversations at Caernef over the years. As a cute child, I played invisibly around the feet of spies, diplomats and assassins, imbibing the atmosphere. As a teenager, I *was* always Miranda, the astute hero, driven and quick-witted, solving mysteries and standing up to queens, kings and governments.

But I can't *be* Miranda when I am *with* Miranda, so sit small, only as Poppy. Poppy Kiwan, the old-fashioned student who grew up out on the clifftop. Poppy Kiwan, who spurns virtuality, who avoids the popular culture of pseudo-identities. Poppy *was* Miranda. Fearless. But now … I am not so sure.

I clutch Arcadian B deep in the pocket of my smart overalls, clinging on to give me courage.

'Hi Poppy, how's it going?' Miranda, lean, immaculate and fragrant, but today looking a tad old and tired. Her piercing eyes capture mine, discerning my thoughts.

'Okay thank you.'

'Good. Follow me into the bowels of Tarquin.' Not disappointed, I tread keenly in her footsteps.

She opens a door, which I had assumed was unused, in a corner of a musty storage room off the vast Tarquin conservatory. It reveals a descending staircase. She checks we are unobserved, and leads the way, closing the door briskly behind us. I follow, using the handrail. Unfamiliar territory for me.

Down two flights, we face a heavy door, bearing a curious handwritten sign saying *Earthworks.* Miranda fishes in her pockets, swears, looks in her shoulder bag, and eventually produces an access card that unlocks the door.

'Open Sesame.' I offer.

'What?'

'Open Sesame. It's from *Ali Baba and the Forty Thieves.* They say it to open the locked door of the cave where the treasure is hidden.' But Miranda is not impressed, so I regret my contribution.

'Hm. No thieves or treasure here Poppy,' she mocks. I remain silent, as we enter a subterranean boardroom. It is *so* Miranda, opulent, sparse. Robin would run a mile from this place. I wait while she fumbles with switches, and then I gasp as an elaborate light show illuminates the white walls. It is as if we are under the ocean, with blue light rippling gently. She activates a soundtrack and the reassuring rhythm of waves fills the room.

'Thought you'd like the show; it's meant to encourage mindfulness.' She smirks, but with no time for mindfulness herself, she switches it off and motions for me to sit at the table, taking the chair opposite me. 'We will meet down here weekly, for a debrief, until the end of your stay. Tell me how's it going?'

Flummoxed, I volunteer, 'It's okay. I seem to be managing the work. Sometimes they have to pull me up on presentation of food when I take a turn in the kitchens. They leave me alone when I'm cleaning. I'm used to cleaning at Caernef. Some people might think it was dull, but it gives me time to think.'

'Hm. And the staff?'

'They are a bit suspicious of me but they're nice enough.'

'The guests?'

'I don't see the guests much.'

'But what have you noticed about them?'

Help! I haven't noticed anything much. Desperate to impress Miranda, I mutter, 'I give them names; I like working on characters. There's a group of three who come in several times a week: The Clinician, The Muddler and the Scurrilous.'

'Ha! Brilliant! Clinician, Muddler and Scurrilous. Poppy, you should work for Nathan.'

Confused, I wait for more.

'I didn't know you were into character. Thought you wanted to be an eco-scientist?'

'Not really …'

'Well?'

'I want to study arts, literature …'

'God, your parents won't like that.'

'You're telling me.'

'Anyway, tell me about the Clinician …'

'He is astute. Always alert. He spends much of his time

on his various devices and avoids eye contact.'

'Yes. You carry on watching him. He doesn't work for us, and I need intelligence. Bide your time. Gain his trust. And The Muddler?'

'Do you know her?' I ask, courageously.

'She isn't what she seems Poppy. Verna, the Muddler, as you call her, works for me. She's a first-class operator. It's all a front. You don't need to worry about her. And The Scurrilous?'

'I can't quite make him out. He's much younger than the other two …'

'Why scurrilous? You've hit the nail on the head there.'

'I don't trust him. He scrabbles in his bag. He's always blowing his nose and leaving for the toilet. His eyes look … devious.'

'Keep him in your sights. I don't know him. He's up to something Poppy, and I need you to find out.'

'Me?' I blurt out before checking myself.

'Yep. You can do it. You look so innocent, but you are as astute as the Clinician. Now, I must dash. We will meet again in the vestibule same time next week. Keep a low profile.' As she rises, accelerating towards the door, she throws a final question at me, which she obviously hopes I will not answer, 'Anything else you need?'

I remain silent as she hustles me back up the two flights of stairs and into the normal world again. All I see is her back view dashing round the corner in a waft of scent, so I return to my duties.

No better than a Victorian scullery maid, after my long domestic shifts, I return to the box room upstairs, sandwiched between linen cupboards. A metre across, I have to sit on the bed to operate, but I'm used to that at home. Trouble is, the pressure of secretly watching strange people in Miranda's orbit is getting to me, and I can't sleep. There are already big black rings under my eyes. Mum would tell me to bathe my face in rosewater, and press slices of bitter home-grown cucumbers on my closed eyes. But there's nothing much like that here, and I haven't ventured out to shops as my meals are all provided downstairs. I can't really smuggle slices of cucumber out of the kitchen. Odd; what I intended to be a bid for freedom has resulted in hard work and a different sort of imprisonment.

In the early hours, I've taken to imagining my routes around Caernef, until sleep finally catches me. It is soothing to be back there. Safe. Reassuring. Who needs Nathan's virtuality, when you have your own in-built imagination? Tonight, I am pulling the duvet around my head, clenching my eyes shut, reluctantly inhaling the vague disinfectant smell that lurks in all the bedding from the bed bug treatments. Ironic how the creatures we want are going extinct, whereas the ones we don't want are proliferating. Anyway, I am going to walk the perimeter of Caernef, in the hope I fall asleep before I complete the circuit.

I am starting at the arcade. My arcade. The tumbledown wooden hut, set against the cliff, which is, externally, exactly as Nathan left it, ten years ago. Perhaps a bit more decayed. Lichen on the timbers and striations of rust on the rainwater tank at the back. Moss overwhelming the roof tiles. I run my fingers across the peeling green paint on the door, hot from the sun. Little flakes of paint float off in the breeze. I actually long for the arcade. Wish I was back there, being my own boss again. I'm not disillusioned by Miranda, just a bit out of my depth and worried I will disappoint her.

I turn my back on the arcade to face the estuary. When I was younger, the air billowing off the sea was fresh and salty, even fishy. Nowadays that same air is strangely warm and stale throughout the year. The ravages of global warming, of course. We didn't heed the warnings quickly enough. It is low tide, my favourite time, so I scramble quickly down the sheep path, brushing my hands across the clumps of scrawny ling, grabbing at tussocky of sea thrift to steady myself. I reach the rocks above the tideline and turn towards Robin's folly. Robin is sometimes out on the rocks, but not this time. I stand still as a stone. There is not a single person within earshot, but the cries of seabirds rise and fall, the background music of my childhood. Always accompanied by the comforting wash of the waves.

Confident in my footing, I scamper across the boulders above the water's edge, where angry waves are asserting their presence. Across the estuary, lorries are grinding up and down to the quarry, but at Caernef, the protected square mile of woodland, cliffs and shoreline, sounds are only natural. Before I reach the jagged monoliths, which skirt the tideline beneath the folly, I remember the peculiar fragment of conversation I overheard while Miranda's targets were waiting for their drinks. Lowering their voices, they definitely said, 'But who will actually press the switch? Not her. Future Proof is her magnum opus, but she will not want her hands tainted with blame. Too risky for *her*. She will get someone else to do it. Who?'

My ears are young and sharp. I'm used to listening for the crack of twigs when I'm out at night tracking badgers and foxes. I can detect the tiniest of rustles that give away birds sitting on eggs. My ears are supreme.

What is a *magnum opus*? Wonder what they meant. *She* is obviously Miranda. Perhaps she will ask me to press *the switch* for her.

But I am on the shore at Caernef, the tide is slowly rising, and I glance up at the dry skirt of green below the folly, edging the top of the rugged cliffs. I stare towards Robin's window, and there she is, with her binoculars; a tiny character in a window, raising her arm, stiffly, as if she is a toy carved from wood. She spots me on the rocks, and I imagine she is smiling.

I'm not going to stop at the folly tonight, so I continue along the shore until I see the gap in the rocks, which only I know. Squeezing through warily, I grip the branches of the scraggy blackthorn, and pull myself up on to the lower path, avoiding most of the prickles. On this lower path I can smell the parched bracken, crunching under my feet. I run. Being Miranda. To my right is the estuary, to my left the steep hillside below The Camp. I quickly reach the barbed wire fencing, which has been stretched across the path. I ignore one of the many brash notices declaring, *Private Property, Caernef Estates controlled by Executive Property Ltd.* I drop back down towards the precarious platform of springy turf hidden in the gorse, then I creep around the blockage. They can't stop me. The Camp may have been outsourced, but in God's eyes this headland is my home.

It occurs to me that the snatched conversation about who might press the switch is similar to the fragments I picked up about the Executive Property takeover a few years ago. No one wanted it to happen, but the debts were growing and, as Mum said, the bureaucracy was stifling. So, the camp and the eco-centre separated. But for me, defining the perimeter with my footsteps, Caernef is all one. As Robin says, she still owns the actual land. They just run the camp. It makes more money now, enabling our side of the clifftop to thrive. We have been able to develop the microgrid, the allotments, install totally better compost toilets and bring back the Eco bus to collect visitors from the station.

At first, I can remain invisible on the path bordering the clifftop below the camp. My regular footfall compacts the mud between the stones. I run. Miranda again. Glancing upwards towards the parade ground, I am forced to deviate from the path to remain incognito. Stealthily progressing through the copse, careful with my feet, picking up beech nuts to stow in my pockets. Through the low branches. Through the low branches.

....

I am dragged awake by banging on the door of my cupboard room. 'Poppy, it's six o'clock!' If I was Miranda, I would swear, turn over and close my eyes again. But I am really Poppy, so I leap up guiltily. Just time to sling on my uniform, rake a comb through the black mat of my hair and bolt out of the door. Not the way to start a day.

…………

Day after day of waitressing, cleaning, stints in the kitchen plating up. I'm bored with it, plus, Miranda's secret work is amounting to nothing much. The Clinician has disappeared, the Muddler woman who, so it seems, works for Miranda anyway, is keeping out of my eyeline, and the Scurrilous is proving elusive. Find out what he is up to, Miranda said. But I'm failing in that task.

…………

'What is *future proof*, Miranda?' I ask again, feigning innocence.

'Well, it depends …'

'Yes?'

'#FutureProof is the latest fad supported by Robin and her cronies, the eco-warriors, out to save the planet.'

'And for you, Miranda?' I ask, looking curiously into her eyes.'

'You're better out of that Poppy!'

'But I'm into it now. I have heard them talk about it, so I know.'

'So?'

'So, I need to know. It isn't just the hashtag, is it? There's something else. That's why I'm working for you here. The Muddler knows about it, and the Clinician is trying to find out …'

Miranda turns to me, and with a weird twinkle in her eye, she scatters clues at my feet, 'Future Proof is about the end of the world as we know it. Imagine starting all over again … just think, Poppy, if humankind could learn from all the mistakes and cock-ups …' She gazes wistfully around the room, adding, 'When you go home to Caernef, ask Robin about *The Return of the Native*. You know, in the parcel you took to her.'

'Why?'

'You'll see. I must dash. Keep up the good work my

little spy!'

4: PIA

An opportunity presents itself when I am least expecting. Just about to take a scheduled break, as I am exiting the opulent Tarquin dining room, I spot the Scurrilous and the Clinician loitering outside on the lawn, their heads close together as if deep in a confidential conversation.

I tread silently past the burdock, to take my break in the fresh air, pausing behind the trunk of the weeping willow tree, where I often see domestic staff like me, lurking anonymously. The bare earth is peppered with cigarette ends.

Straining my ears, all I can hear is their mumbling voices. Disappointed. About to give up when, by chance, they stroll in my direction. I am totally concealed. Reminds me of stalking deer in the woodlands behind Caernef. For a moment in time, reality is suspended. I am completely fixed on these two dodgy characters; Miranda's current targets. Desperate to obtain a morsel of intelligence to please her, I freeze. Listen intently.

The Clinician is frustrated, 'Their fucking Future Proof is a joke. What *she* is trying to do is *impossible*.'

The Scurrilous is scheming, 'But our Future Proof will win through. Just you wait and see. They all believe they are on the trip to the future, them with their chosen few. But Reginald has it in hand. They will go down with the rest of the world. Annihilation. Day Zero … my arse. Our seats are booked sir. Our seats are booked.'

The Clinician mutters, 'I hope you're right my friend,' and they saunter on to the gravel path, out of earshot. I remain incognito. Am I being Miranda? Am I really her little spy?

I save this tasty morsel until my final rendezvous with Miranda, down in the sleazy depths of Tarquin.

'So Poppy Kiwan, what have you to report before you return home?' It's a child's game for her. She has been testing me, I know this now: Miranda, the queen bee, has simply been checking my loyalty, checking my discretion.

'I overheard the Clinician and the Scurrilous.'

'Go on …'

'They said that #FutureProof was rubbish, that Reginald had it all in hand, and that they were on the trip to the future.'

'Really?'

'Yes; I am sure. I was behind the big willow tree while they walked on the gravel path. I could hear that very clearly. No doubt, Miranda.'

'Surely not *Reginald*?'

I have heard of Miranda and Robin's grandfatherly mentor, Reginald De Vere, many times, but never met him. He doesn't visit Caernef. Every Christmas he sends Robin books tied with ribbons and wrapped in expensive paper.

'Maybe it's a different Reginald?' I offer.

'I doubt it. Are you sure? Anything else?' She wrinkles her forehead, checking her watch.

'They made fun of Day Zero, and scoffed at *annihilation*. That was it.'

'Did they now, and what do they know about *day zero* I wonder?'

'I am beginning to understand what this is all about. Your #FutureProof, Miranda, secures the future of the planet. You are obtaining global diplomatic agreements. But they are out to stop you. They want the future for themselves, and your so-called Reginald is helping them.

He's the double-crosser Miranda.' I look at the floor. Maybe I have said too much. I play Miranda at her own game with directness cloaking subterfuge. Feigning confidence, I ask her, 'Have I passed your tests? Do I get to move to the next level?'

'Of course. I've enjoyed our little chats. It's been nice having you here rather than buried in the cul-de-sac of Caernef. You will come back, won't you? Christmas holidays? Tarquin is always looking for extra staff?'

I think of my bank balance. Higher than ever, due to four weeks slaving in Oxfordshire, pretending to be older than I am. I think of the tired Christmas customs at home, the smallness of it. 'Yes, of course.'

'A car will arrive at nine next Monday morning to take you to the station. Safe journey Poppy. Give my love to your mum and dad. To Cai.'

'And to Robin?'

'Ha! Tell her there's still a place for her if she wants it.'

'A place?'

'You know, on the trip to the future.'

'Robin is getting old and tired. She says she is too tired for the future.'

'Poppycock.'

Miranda sails up the stairs, with me trailing in her wake. Before accelerating out into the driveway, she turns and winks at me. I'm well-in with my hero right now.

…………

After work on Saturday, hiding comfortably in my broom cupboard, reading *Where the Crawdads Sing* for at least the tenth time, I pick up a cryptic message from Cai on my outdated phone, *log in you're there!*

As I have no way of logging in myself, I ignore the message. I'm heading home on Monday, and he can show me what he means. I'm actually looking forward to the familiarity of seeing Cai, even squashing into the small bed in our tiny shared bedroom. Anything will be better than the domestic incarceration of the memorable Tarquin broom cupboard. My summer holiday job has run its course, and I have earnt more than ever before. I did odd jobs at Caernef for pocket money, but Tarquin has provided a grand salary, although I have made no friends here, and I have hardly seen Miranda.

Another message from Cai, *your awesome.* I can only assume he means 'you're'. Smile, turn off the phone and return to my book.

....

The final few Tarquin days drag. It is with immense relief that I throw my uniform into the dirty laundry, scour the broom cupboard to check I have left nothing behind, and return my access pass to reception. Harvey even takes the trouble to find me before I leave, handing me a card with a delightful picture of wild flowers on the front, signed by many of the staff.

'All the best Poppy,' he says, 'Come back at Christmas. There's a job for you at Tarquin if you want it!' What a surprise.

....

Cai has actually come out to the station with Dad to collect me. Their joy at seeing me arrive home again is touching, but all they can talk about is virtuality.

'Haven't you seen it yet Pops?'

'Even I am impressed. You never said anything. How did you keep it a secret?' Dad is not a virtuality fan, but he dabbles during dark evenings when outdoor work is more difficult. They rattle on.

'Nathan has relocated you, but we *know*. Anyone who is familiar with Caernef will *know*. It's so true to life. How does he do it?'

I can bear it no longer. 'What? I don't have any idea what you are talking about?'

Silence. Puzzled faces. The car draws into the bottom car park at Caernef. Dad turns to me, checking, nervously, 'You don't know about this?'

Their faces drop as they assume my answer. With an

upbeat note, Cai says he will show me. As we return to the cottage, which seems so tiny after only a few weeks away, Mum fusses around me. Her usually luscious hair is lank, and she stoops as if she carries a huge weight on her shoulders. Despite her downbeat look, she is obviously overjoyed to see me.

Before I have even unpacked, Cai rushes me upstairs, planting me on his bed with the virtuality screen directly in front of us. He activates the game, we listen to the haunting opening music, then, suddenly, there I am. Unmistakeably me. Three-dimensional and … meek, vulnerable … innocent-looking.

'I can enter your identity 'cos I have reached the higher levels,' he explains, 'but most people will see you externally and play you that way.'

Totally devastated I ask, nervously, 'Is it … am I … called Poppy?'

'No! Look, here, the character is Pia. Just Pia. No other names. Simple and effective.'

'Pia. Means pious,' I offer nervously.

'That figures. Nathan has an amazing brain.'

This new avatar, Pia, is a detailed hand-drawn virtuality replica of me. Short, stocky, unassuming. My black hair. My dark eyes. My dimple, accentuated. Even wearing my clothes. An old jersey, which I still use, along with my favourite leggings. Boots.

I never wanted to become a super-hero. I never wanted to use virtuality let alone feature in it. Fighting the temptation to become distraught, I ask Cai, 'This Pia, she is a minor character? Just one choice for players, out of hundreds, right?'

Cai sends me a withering look. 'Pia is THE character. The new release for 2034. Everyone wants Pia. She is capturing the hearts of players worldwide. Just wait until you see her in action.'

'Cai, I'm not sure …'

But it is too late, as Cai flicks open a clifftop scene, and

Pia jogs with my tentative, loping style, along my paths, past my wildlife, pausing to examine a butterfly, scampering across the heather, clambering over rocks. 'Does virtuality name Caernef?' I splutter, devastated by the likeness.

'No. We're safe. The location is disclosed as somewhere in the wilds of the north of Scotland. He has even added a twang to your accent. Nathan is too canny to put us at risk, and he doesn't want another interminable battle with Robin's lawyers.'

We watch in silence. Cai operates me, I mean Pia, I mean … she is running back across the clifftop, with echoes of Celtic singing in the background, stopping outside the door of *the arcade*, panting lightly, just like I do. What the hell is going on here? The peeling green paint. The exact door.

'Shall we go in?' Cai asks keenly, misinterpreting my awestruck look as something positive.

'Yes,' I manage to blurt out.

Pia opens the door with her right hand. I always use my left. Stubbornly left-handed. Nathan has consciously switched this; I wonder why.

And there is the cyber-junk, there are my specimens, my paintings, all on display for the world to scrutinise, my private and most precious world. Cai manoeuvres the character towards the back of the shed. 'I've been here before Pops, look.' He shows me Nathan's glowing platform, the greenish blue radiance of the filaments. It was my secret … I thought. Now the whole world knows. Pia pauses in front of it.

'What is she going to do now?' I gasp.

'Look, it's exquisite.' Cai moves Pia's virtual fingers, grasps the handle on Nathan's old workbench, manipulating it to and fro to an expectant cello accompaniment. 'It's two turns to the right with a half turn back. Took me ages to solve that one. Now, what would you like to transform today? There's loads to choose from;

birds, butterflies, ancient fossils. They could all come back to life.'

'I … I … Cai, you choose.'

Through the avatar, he picks up *my* swallowtail butterfly, brittle from years in *my* collection tin, places it on to the platform. Slowly, with sparkles, glockenspiel and digital rainbows, it comes to life, landing on Pia's outstretched hand.

'Wow.'

…………

'We thought you were in on it,' Mum thumps a mug of tea down in front of me. The family table is not harmonious this evening.

Dad tries to calm the atmosphere, 'You must admit, it's exquisitely drawn. It captures your wildness, your odd combination of nervousness and awkward cheek.'

'Cheek?' I challenge Dad, my confused feelings boiling over.

'You know, Anyway, at least it is a high-quality product.'

'It's fantastic to play,' Cai adds.

I appeal to Mum, who is slamming about in the kitchen, chinking plates unnecessarily, 'Mum, it's not right, is it?'

'Well, Poppy, whether it is right or not, it is out there, everywhere, and we will have to deal with it. Now, try to explain why it is upsetting you *so* much.'

'Because … because my life is my own, not some game to be played by millions of ogling voyeurs. Because all that was quietly private to me is now on show. Some girl called Pia has taken over who I am, in every minute detail, without me even knowing. I'm angry, beyond angry, at the injustice. I need a lawyer. It has ruined my life. Forever.'

'Hey darling, calm down, Dad tries to comfort me, adding, 'On a practical note, if you weren't aware of any of this, how did Nathan and his damned virtuality do it?'

'I'd like to know,' Mum growls.

'But Nathan is a good chap,' Cai intervenes, 'let's just ask him.' Cai taps on his phone, messages Nathan, expecting a reply. We drink our tea in silence. Compared with the immense dining room at Tarquin, our tiny kitchen feels like something from history. The small range, the sooty grease, cupboards with doors that have never closed properly, and the heap of boots by the back door. Crumbs of mud spilling across the flagstones. That is why Nathan's use of *me* is so compelling. Not many people live in the past nowadays. The real-life generations are either too old, or have died. Devices have become the norm. I am an anachronism, but I don't want to be a spectacle.

Cai's phone pings. 'Ah, good for Nathan. He generally responds to me. Ah, yes, he says, *just wait for Pia II*, they are working on it at the moment, and it's even better.'

'Damn Pia II, what does he say about me?' I demand.

Cai taps again, receiving an instant response, 'Nathan says it's all in the contract, and not to worry, the royalties will be significant.'

'What contract?' We shout, simultaneously.

Mum and Dad exchange looks. 'There was a contract?' I ask, icily.

'It was years ago, just after Nathan had left. He said it was to safeguard your interests, and as you were only a child, we signed for you. He reassured us that if there was any profit, you would be entitled to a share. This was long before he made such a success of virtuality.'

I don't stay to hear any more. I slam my tea on the table, shouting, 'I don't want any … royalties!' Their confused eyes follow me as I leave.

The most sensible thing to do is to head for Robin. She has plenty of experience of unwanted fame, of contracts and game-playing. Robin will completely understand my wrath. But Robin is like an aged aunt past her best. I need someone strong behind me right now.

My parents' words, 'How did Nathan do it?' ring in my head. Standing on the cliff edge, gasping the air in an attempt to wash away my panic, I realise Nathan and his well-paid tech friends are somehow tracking me even now.

Miranda. Yes; Miranda would say, 'Look like you're playing their game Poppy, but play your own game. Take charge. You can turn this to your advantage.' So, thanks to Miranda, I take myself in hand, return to the cottage, apologise to my parents, make peace with Cai, play the whole thing down, and get some sleep.

In the split second before I fall into oblivion, I hear Dad say to Mum, 'Best not to tell her about the social media.' It's inevitable I suppose. There are many unforgiving and bitter people out there who will launch their invective at this manifestation of me. Not going to let that stop me sleeping. Tough like Miranda.

…………

As is usual when I'm home, I creep out early, before anyone else is up. I set off for the arcade in glorious late summer sunshine. No doubt some low-paid virtuality trackers are fixed to the screen right now, stalking me, so I loop and spin, creating chaos for their entertainment. Then I head for Nathan's platform, where, without hesitation, I place a fragile skeleton of a grasshopper on to the plate, and, just as Cai described, twist the handle twice to the right and a half-turn back.

Nothing happens.

That's tested that then. They are making things up. Okay.

…………

It's early Sunday morning: Robin and I are the only people up and about. We are enjoying the cacophony of birdsong. I found her sitting on the old bench outside the folly, staring towards the estuary. As I sat next to her, she beamed at me; one of her rare radiant smiles.

'Poppy: the person who I most love to see on an early morning. Tell me, what can you see out on the water today?'

Despite her glasses, Robin's eyes will only be seeing

blue-grey swirls in the distance, so I describe the scene for her. The emerging rays of September sun catching the gentle ripples, the gulls squabbling on the rocks, a shag standing majestically, his wings drying in the sunlight. Caernef at its very best.

She sighs, 'Caernef was my dream, but … it has become a heavy weight on my shoulders. It has become my indulgence …'

I stare at her withered face, all veins and blotches, her melancholy eyes and her swollen knuckles, wondering how Caernef has become an indulgence, so I ask her.

'I was dragged into stopping the glitch, all those years ago, and, along with my friends, I created #isolate, we masterminded #Spoiler. We saved the world from vicious cyber-terrorists. We changed the future path of a nation. We offered dispersed communities a common purpose, and they rose to the challenge. But now, I am nothing …'

'But Future Proof is your current project. #FutureProof trends month after month. There is a huge following. People want to save the planet. They still do.'

'You think so, Poppy? Do you really think so?'

'Of course.'

'But I fear it is becoming too late. The young people spend far more time gaming on their phones than in real life. Of course, I was youthful and naïve once, but I harboured impressive ideals, lived by my principles, believing in change, just as you do. However, nowadays I am in pain. Weak from pathetic efforts that are, essentially, outdated.'

'How do you mean Robin?' I coax.

'I mean that I am a feeble anachronism, with agony in my limbs. With failing eyesight. Before my time. Look at me; I can't even live independently out here now. I struggle to get up and down the stairs. My fibromyalgia isn't going to get any better. From now on, it's only going to be uphill. I have missed the time to act. I might be too late.' She focuses on me, and switches into a less deterministic mode, 'You represent the future. Poppy, your generation must act on behalf of people like me.'

'What must we do? I'm not typical. I'm a bit of an outsider. I hate going to school and my classmates don't like me. They all live through Nathan's virtuality.'

'Outsiders are the interesting ones. People who buck the trend. Mavericks and trailblazers.'

The shag shakes its wings, flaps clumsily into the air, then after a few hundred meters, plunges like an arrow deep into the sparkling water, emerging far away towards the opposite bank. Robin laughs, gently.

'I once saw a heron by the river. The first time I met Nathan … You know what to do, Poppy, to #FutureProof the planet? Give these birds and poor but magnificent creatures a chance. Persuade all the virtuality addicts to help you to turn the tide. Forget Miranda, her subterfuge and plotting. She is a survivor, unlike me. She is inherently selfish, and seeks to turn the slow extinction of the planet to her advantage. Forget her, Poppy. Don't get me wrong; I love her dearly, as a … sister. But she is not to be trusted.' Robin glares into the distance.

'I don't understand how you can love and despise her all at once.'

'I think maybe you do understand. All I'm saying is be careful.'

She rises to her feet with effort, sending me on my way. I turn as the clifftop path dives behind the gorse, while she is still standing, staring across the water. Bereft. Makes me want to take on #FutureProof and make a success of it for her. Maybe that should be Pia's next move. Nathan has millions of human beings on board already. I should have asked Robin about Pia, but the moment wasn't right, and she was distracted by her own worries. I'll just have to rely on Miranda for advice.

As I march along the path, I call Miranda to mind. Focusing on her face, I try to get inside her thoughts. I put aside people's misgivings about her, even put aside my childhood memories of her working for the enemy. *Miranda, what should I do?*

What exactly do you want to achieve?

Great; she is there. *Miranda, I need your help.*

Do my best. Spell it out.

Okay: I'm stuck with all the things I don't want. And now, Nathan has recreated my identity in virtuality, the virtuality I have avoided all these years, without my knowledge. Apparently, there was a contract. Worst thing is that Pia, my avatar, is stunning. Alluring. But it means I'm being tracked. Everywhere I go. I'm being turned into virtuality. I'm trapped Miranda. Trapped in so many ways.

Ah, I do trapped Poppy …

I'm trapped at Caernef. Yes, it is beautiful; one of the few truly wild and authentic places around. But I have grown up in a sheltered anachronism. I want to be out in the real world.

Wasn't Tarquin the real world?

Yes. No. It was, but it was a different sort of prison. It was work, work, work, and I had no transport. I felt trapped there.

You have legs?

What?

Legs. You, Poppy, are the ultimate runner. Young Fit. I envy you.

What? Really!

Stop being the victim. Take control. Necessary in the adult world. Don't wait to be told.

I tried with my college courses. I wanted to do arts. But ended up doing sciences. Trapped in that too.

You make yourself trapped. Find a way out. Change courses before it's too late. Go to the college principal if you have to. Agency Poppy. Agency.

Agency?

Take control. Don't let them *push you around.*

Can I do it on my own though Miranda?

Of course you can. Anyway, you aren't alone. You have me at your back. The two of us can tackle anything thrown at us. You know that. Be me Poppy. Be me again. Not Robin, miss goody two-shoes all nice and kind. Be me.

I thank my imaginary mentor, resolving to be better. To do better. To be stronger. Today, I am Miranda. I run the circuit at speed, returning to the arcade to make a plan. Nathan can't get inside my head, only my body. Agency: take control. Miranda is right, as always.

5: GEOTRACKER

Despite Miranda's imaginary words, I know I can't do this alone. It's too big for me, but deciding who to trust makes my head ache. Miranda, of course, says trust no one, but I need a co-conspirator. A friend. A partner. Someone on my level. I need a person who doesn't bring complications with them. There's no one at school. They are too wrapped up in virtuality.

Watching a parliament of magpies high in the branches of the oak trees beside the parade ground. They bicker and caw. One for sorrow, two for joy. Four of the bombastic birds soar down to peck at some debris from the fire pit. It is as if they are looking at me before they dip their heads, scrabbling in the grass for tasty scraps. I am not fond of magpies. Predators. But four for a boy. Thanks magpies; you have decided for me. If it backfires, I will blame you.

Never difficult to hunt down Cai. When he's not at school, he's generally in the bedroom in front of his screens. I usually end up the willing dogsbody, while he rarely helps in the allotments or with the chores. Nobody minds because he is cheerful as well as uncomplicated.

Cai.

I leave my boots outside the back door, avoid Mum and Dad, then pad quickly upstairs. My brother is deep in virtuality; the alluring minor keys of Pia's music fill the room. He holds a finger to his lips as I creep in, flashing me a smile, patting the empty perch beside him.

Cai understands Pia best. Arguably better than Nathan. He manipulates her with ease, seeing out of her eyes.

'I'm determined to get to Pia II first.'

'I don't think Nathan has finished writing it yet.

'Shh Pops …'

I close my eyes patiently while he finishes the level. He's fair, and doesn't start the next one, despite desperately wanting to, before asking me what I want. We've always done that.

'Cai, I need your help.'

'Of course, I'll do my best for you. What is it this time?'

'I … it's … I would like you to help me sort it out. Please Cai. I can't do it on my own, and you are the only person who I can trust with it all.'

Cai puts down his controller, swinging round to face me, a patient smile on his face. 'You know I'll help, but what is it you need me to do?'

I take a deep breath and let it all come tumbling out: Miranda, Robin, Nathan, Pia, #FutureProof, the end of the world. Saving the planet. Saving nature. The curlew and the butterflies. Rising above virtuality. Making a difference.

Cai is old for his thirteen years. His voice has become so deep that I am in awe. He even has a virtual girlfriend, called Ciel. 'You mustn't tell anybody. Not Ciel, certainly not Mum or Dad, certainly not a hint of it in virtuality. It's far too serious.'

Cai rummages in a drawer of his overbed desk, pulls out Chap, a small ragged character wearing a battered cloth hat, and sits him on my knee. It is several years since we have used Chap, but Cai has a knack of knowing the right thing to do at the right time. He takes on a serious air, announcing, 'I swear on Chap's life that I will not speak of this to anyone else. It's just you and me. Like it used to be!' He grins with anticipation.

I seize the moment, 'So we start now. Right now. You come down to the arcade with me and take a look at what

Nathan left behind.'

'With ten years of dust on it.'

'Yes.'

There is something hugely reassuring about walking down to the arcade next to Cai rather than alone. I lead the way inside, heading straight for the platform, take off the oilcloth, and ask him, 'How does it work?'

A beautiful thinking silence engulfs the ramshackle interior of the arcade as Cai, wide-eyed, gazes upon the luminescent green webs, which I have hidden for so long, but that he has seen so recently in virtuality. He places his hand on the lever, raising his eyebrows at me. I nod. He twists the handle twice to the right, and then a half-turn back.

I suddenly feel a stabbing pain in the top of my arm. The spasm grows in intensity. I tear at my sleeve, almost fainting from the pain. 'Turn it back Cai. Turn it back.'

'Hey. Pops, you alright? What the hell was that?'

....

Nathan's communicator bleeps. It is Handsome, one of the senior programmers. *Need to talk right now.* Nathan takes off his headset, calmly hangs his miniscule microphone on his floating desk-light, and heads for the control room.

Handsome beckons to Nathan to come outside with him, on to the fresh-air balcony. The junior programmers scuttle back inside with their coffees. Handsome secures the door. 'She severed the link boss. Suddenly she was gone. She's still gone. Over the years, you said it might happen. Well man, it's happened just now. First time ever. We've totally lost her. I mean she's gone AWOL for a few days, but it's never felt as final as this. All retrieval systems are down this time. Gone'

'Have we got enough data to push ahead with Pia III?'

'Maybe. What you worrying about boss?'

'I don't want her to have died.'

Handsome detects uncharacteristic emotion on the

usually serenely detached face of his mentor and has the sense not to pursue this. 'I'll let you know if … as soon as … she comes back.'

'Yes. Yes please. You do that.'

They return to the lab. Handsome logs back in, as Nathan wanders, stunned, towards the exit, but Handsome catches him as he passes, whispering, urgently, 'It's okay. She's back. Must have been a glitch.'

They grin. 'Don't scare me like that again!' Nathan jests.

…………

But in the privacy of his control room, as Nathan logs back in, he is concerned at the degree of trembling affecting his hands.

On his multiple screens, Pia is running. She runs from the Arctic circle to the equator, from all points of the compass, and spanning the socio-economic spectrum. He thinks of Pia running across screens in cramped bedsits, in opulent bedrooms and in the hands of gamers on benches. Pia is everywhere. The now top-of-the-charts bittersweet melody accompanying her wherever she runs.

She has quickly become an unassuming heroine for the younger generation, a captivating idol, an enigmatic alter-ego, a daughter for the childless and, for the technophobes, an echo of what might have been. Pia has become a living memory for older people, gaming alone in their retirement homes. She has also become a butt for the venom of trolls. Online bullies showing their ignorance. No mercy.

Pia. Pious. Demure, but with a dark smoke in her wide eyes. Alluring. Representing an innocence that has long been lost.

Who Do You Think You Are, Pia? Parentless, homeless, and quietly proud. Without a back story, simply Pia. Roaming the wilderness, wherever Nathan directs, and wherever the gamers take her.

Nathan loves his creation, Pia, with an intense

infatuation. She is both the little sister he never had, and an inaccessible lover, hiding behind the screen. All his devotion has been invested in the creation of this sublime character. He has crafted her as simultaneously enticing, with a touch of belligerence. For Nathan, Pia represents small people in a glorious clash of opposites. Both timid and brave, quiet yet feisty, endowed with the beauty of youth, yet unaware. Innocence with a tinge of worldliness. Emerging but not yet there.

His team of animators have captured the very essence of Poppy, exactly as he instructed, rebranding her as Pia. Finally, when Nathan was satisfied, having swept away his nagging doubts about integrity, and only then, did he give the okay to launch. Persuading himself that Pia is ethical, justifying his product as the ultimate weapon in the battle for #FutureProof. He is hoping Pia will headline as the most successful eco-character of 2034. Robin won't acknowledge the success, but through Pia, he can, at least, contribute to her cause. Nathan has been watching #FutureProof from afar and is poised to invest more than his expertise in character design. The years he spent at Caernef have imprinted deeply within him a lasting devotion to the land. He may be the master of virtuality, but he will never lose touch with the clifftop, the allotments and the low-tech community in which he spent his early twenties.

He thinks of Cai, who is not only growing into a serious young man deserving of attention, but is also an ardent devotee of virtuality. Nathan is flattered. Cai evokes memories of long summer walks, roaming the paths around Caernef, when Nathan carried the little fellow on his back. 'I'll take him for a walk Maria.' In those bygone days, Nathan chatted away to Cai, telling him of his dreams, out in the crystal-clear clifftop air. Cai chortled, six months old, enjoying Nathan's companionship.

But the crystal-clear air is no more, out at Caernef, and Pia is running.

From the moment Nathan, personally, finally tapped the *live* key, Pia has been running. Poppy's alter-ego. But Poppy didn't know. This slight lack of transparency irks Nathan. It sours his perfect creation. Some nights, he secretly wishes Poppy would die. It is possible he has all the data he needs. Pia is the real character now. In fact, some nights Nathan wishes the real world would expire, as people keep predicting, so virtuality would become the new world. But that's impossible. Of course.

Nathan is lonely. Followed by billions, and surrounded by passionate employees, colleagues, ardent customers, keen investors and aspirant entrepreneurs, he has never felt so alone. He hides a gaping hole deep inside his being, which is causing him pain. Some days his head feels as if it will explode with the pressure of the sheer volume of virtuality. Nathan, listed amongst the wealthiest, with a packed diary, and the necessity of cherry-picking his meetings. In demand. Non-stop.

However, for the first time today, Nathan has been scared into realising how dependent he is on Poppy. Was it only a glitch? If so, he must #stoptheglitch. Again. Or is there trouble at Caernef? Is Poppy in trouble?

…………

I shyly show Cai the place in my arm where Nathan's miniscule implant is lodged deep under the surface of my skin.

'Is it safe?' He asks me.

'It's not been any trouble for ten years. Not until just then. It's fine now. Cai, do you think there is a connection between my geotracker and the platform?'

'There must be. I can't believe you told nobody about this Pops.'

'I forgot about it to be honest.'

'Like Mum and Dad forgot Nathan's contract. We need to speak to Nathan.'

'No.'

'No?'

'He has not trusted or respected me and I no longer trust him. We need to find out how it all works and put an end to it. I want my life back.'

'You're not saying we somehow crash the whole of Pia I? But it is brilliant. Absolutely brilliant.'

'Right now, Cai, I want to crash the whole of virtuality. Like Miranda, I want to wipe out all the unhealthy human obsessions so we can return to zero again. Start again and do better. Care for the planet I mean. Do all the things we didn't realise we had to do to keep our life on earth a safe, healthy one.'

'That's too big for me to get my head around. Where do we start. Let's get down to practicalities.'

I cover the glowing platform with the oilcloth, and we perch on Nathan's old bench, staring at the conglomeration of outdated cyber junk alongside my collections of stones, fossils, feathers and nuts, all sorted and labelled, but all dead. I glance out of the cracked glass, keen to see living wildlife I hear a characteristic squeal.

'Look Cai!'

'I can't see anything.'

'Come outside quietly.' I lead him stealthily out on to the platform of thrift.

'You move just like Pia'

'Shh no: she moves like me,' I whisper. 'Over there, look now.'

I know it is a white-tailed eagle; sometimes called a sea eagle. I have only seen it a few times, but I am sure. The majestic bird is in freefall, its feathers ragged in the wind. It skims the water, lunges, and soars off into the distance with booty in its talons.

'Wow.'

'See Cai: that's a million times better than virtuality. The real thing. Do you know, sea eagles were extinct, and now they are back, after breeding programmes. That is what we should be doing with our lives, giving nature a helping hand, using our technology to protect the planet, rather than all this endless and pointless entertainment.'

'How often do you see them down here?'

'Very rarely. You are lucky.'

'Perhaps it is a sign.'

'Is it? You'll have to look out for the appearance of a sea eagle in Pia II.' I add with a wry grimace.

'So, you are telling me that Nathan has built Pia's virtuality platform through the transponder in your arm, and the glowing thing in the arcade is his means of linking to the transponder? You are saying that Nathan is tracing your every move, reproducing the best bits in his cyber games?'

'I suppose so.'

'He knows you come to the arcade most days, every day, except when you were away with Miranda. Don't you think it's too late? Nathan will have harvested enough data to run Pia I, II and III at least.'

'What if we subvert it from within Cai? What if I play the game myself? After all, I know my character better than anyone, so should be able to progress really quickly once I get the hang of it. When I'm well-into it, we could start creating the story for Nathan to write. Set him up.'

'I thought you hated virtuality.'

'I do, but this is different. I'm desperate.'

'Okay, happy to give it a try.'

I lock the arcade, although it is so ramshackle; someone with a screwdriver or a saw could be inside in minutes. We walk home. I relax, knowing we have a plan, and I'm not alone any more.

....

'Poppy!' Mum is shouting for me before I am even awake.

'Poppy, come here!'

'What? I'm not dressed yet.'

'Robin's supper is still here on the table. You didn't take it up to the folly last night. She will have gone hungry, and be worrying. What were you thinking of?'

Damn. I've never forgotten before. That's virtuality for

you. Cai spent the evening teaching me the moves and we carried on until so late, I fell asleep. Poor Robin. I feel terrible. Throw some clothes over my pyjamas and even grovel to Mum.

'It was all my fault. Cai was showing me virtuality and we got well-into it. I'm so sorry Mum.'

'It's Robin you should say sorry to.'

'Why didn't she phone us?'

'You know Robin, not wanting to be any trouble. I hope you are going to head up there right away.'

'Yes. I'm sorry Mum.'

'Here, take this. At least she can have a hot breakfast. She is fading away in that folly of hers.'

Mum wraps her own uneaten breakfast in foil. I take it and run. The outside world feels different this morning. It is as if the sky, the clouds and the plants are mourning my conversion to virtuality. I try to explain to them as I run through the light drizzle, melancholy in the slanted sunshine.

'Robin!' I call, banging on the door. 'Robin, I'm so sorry …'

No reply.

'Hi; Robin!'

No Robin. The folly is in darkness. Perhaps she has gone out, but she never goes far these days. I walk the perimeter of the folly, peering in the kitchen window. Everything looks tidy, but I can see no sign of Robin. I lay the pathetic foil parcel on the doorstep, in case she comes down, and run, frantically back home. A solitary magpie flaps over the parade ground as I stumble by, working out what to say to Mum. I burst into the kitchen, smelling Dad's strong coffee, and plump for, 'I left it on the step. There's no sign of her. Maybe she's still asleep,' adding, 'Mum, I think we had better go back and check. It didn't feel right down there.'

'I could do without any extra trouble this morning. Thomas, love, can you go to check on Robin? No supper was delivered last night. I've sent breakfast but Poppy can't raise her.'

Dad finds the spare key to the folly, and I hurry behind him as he marches purposefully along the path. I realise I haven't brushed my hair or eaten anything. This is not how I intended to start my day.

He unlocks and … almost falls over Robin. She is lying motionless at the foot of the stairs. I feel faint with shock.

'Poppy, have you got your phone?'

'No, Dad. Sorry.'

'Shit. Neither have I. Right, you run back to Mum. Get her to call the paramedics right away.' He sounds so calm, but that's my dad for you. Calm under pressure. Reliable. Kind. Just as I am about to leg it to get help, the motionless figure groans. Robin opens her eyes and croaks, 'Thomas?'

'Hang on Poppy, I might need you here,' Dad calls.

With a gargantuan effort, Robin raises her head from the floor, holds a withered arm out towards Dad, letting him help her into a sitting position on the bottom step.

'I'm okay,' she insists, pulling her dressing gown round her and smiling through her shivers. 'I'm okay. Don't worry. I must have tripped on the stairs and hit my head, but I feel fine now.'

She is regaining some colour to her cheeks. Despite the drama, Dad sounds relaxed, 'You gave us a fright there, Robin. Now, let's check you over.'

'I will refuse to go with any paramedics, even though they are good people. I will downright refuse. You know I will.'

Dad raises his eyebrows in my direction, 'What are we going to do with you! Poppy, make Robin a cup of tea and sit with this obstinate woman while I fetch Mum.'

'I'm so sorry I forgot your supper. This is all my fault.'

'Supper? Oh, that was fine, I had some leftover soup. This is not your fault at all. I must have tripped on the stairs. Stupid me.'

I brew tea, throwing in some sugar, passing a steaming mug to Dad. He walks back to the kitchen, adds cold water, and returns to Robin, who is now sitting on the bottom step, bedraggled but very much alive.

'Sip your tea and tell me if it hurts anywhere. Your head?'

Robin considers this, feels her arms, her legs, and her forehead. 'I think I bumped my forehead here, and this ankle hurts, but that's all. I'll live.'

A bump is coming up on her forehead. I fetch Mum's witch hazel from the kitchen, anoint her head, then find a bag of frozen Caernef peas, telling her to hold it on the bump. I have watched Mum administer the same remedy to Cai many times. He was much more active as a young boy, always getting into scrapes. Before virtuality took over.

By the time Mum arrives, hassled and concerned, I have discovered Robin's twisted ankle, moving the peas down there. Robin is telling me all about the sea eagle, which she now remembers she saw from her lookout. She was hurrying downstairs to get a closer look from the clifftop. That is why she fell.

'More haste less speed,' she laughs, putting on a show for Mum, proving she is okay. Mum calls her incorrigible, rescues the breakfast from the step, makes sure Robin is able to walk, then bandages her twisted ankle. What a scare.

As we leave, promising to come back and check on her later this morning, Robin hobbles outside to sit on the bench and look for the sea eagle. She calls me back, and I perch next to her.

'I want you to know Poppy; when I die, the folly will be yours. No one else loves Caernef as you do. You are the original child of Caernef. It's only right that you should inherit my folly. But as long as I am still alive and kicking, I will not budge. Now, pop into the kitchen, there's a dear. Fetch me a glass of water and some painkillers. They are hidden right at the back of the cutlery drawer. Don't tell your mum; she prefers me to take herbal remedies!'

I find them for her, squirrelled away out of sight, wondering what else she hides from Mum.

'Now, run along Poppy. Maybe I'll see you later.'

I sprint after Mum, secretly feeling ungrateful. I don't want to be incarcerated in the folly at Caernef with all its history and memories. I want to escape. Robin is so kind, but the very thought of her not being there, in the folly, and of me taking her place, fills me with dread. I have never *been* Robin, only Miranda. It just wouldn't be right.

6: GID

We're back in the routine of school, and I am ploughing through the sciences. Not what I want to be studying. I live for after school, and being home at Caernef.

Tonight, it is raining heavily outside, so Cai is operating while I am advising. Pia is running. This time, heading for the ruined Castle of Ceòlm, to a gothic background track. She is looking for the secret of the whin. If she finds it, Cai will be able to enter the next level, which might be Pia II. Not only am I enjoying the game, against my best instincts, but I am in tune with Pia. I know where she needs to go, and what she needs to do, despite diving into the middle of the game rather than starting from the beginning.

'Cai, you could be looking for a gorse bush. That's the *whin.*'

'Gorse?'

'Where have you been? You know; prickly bushes with yellow flowers. They grow all around here, and no doubt in virtuality too. Look for a gorse bush, but there won't be any in this foreboding jungle. We need to get out on to a heath or plain.'

Pia runs on through the depths of the forest of Ceòlm. The dim light makes it hard to discern more than shadows. Sweeping branches trip her. Tangled ivy and a wild honeysuckle, which I call woodbine, brushes across her face, adventure echoing in the soundtrack. Pia is running, but I have slipped into her persona, so sweetly. *I* am running.

In the forest, eyes blink in the canopy, perched on branches, lurking in the undergrowth, but I do not fear them, because I am used to Caernef. The path is rocky, so I rely on surefooted agility to maintain my speed. I need to find a way out of the dense tree cover. Stop and listen. Very faint splashing of water, far in the distance.

I grab the controller from Cai.

'Hey, what are you doing?'

'We need to follow the water, Cai. Water will lead us out into the open.' At the moment I am in control, and Cai is the observer. Having located the stream, I track the watercourse uphill, skipping across the shale, holding my feet firm, not slipping. The rushing water soon becomes a trickle, the trees open out, and I am surrounded by scrubby bushes. A magnificent blue sky appears over my head.

'Watch out!'

Cai grabs the controller. I was naïve, as, once out from cover, I am spotted by a hoard of seemingly malevolent spirits. They are cloaked in grey, with human faces and long wispy hair, but on all-fours, reminiscent of William Blake's Nebuchadnezzar.

'They are only wylver. I've beaten them before.' Cai reassures me, but as he adeptly manipulates Pia's bow and arrow, poised to fire, I intervene.

'No! I wouldn't do that. Hold on Cai. Hold on …'

Reluctantly, he hands the controller back. I lay down my bow and arrow.

'That's suicide, Poppy. We'll have to start the level all over again …'

Cai and I could fall out over this, but my instinct pays off. I approach the wylver, in friendship. There are at least thirty of them, ranging from huge hairy-faced creatures to soft-skinned youngsters, with wide eyes. The leader, a terrifyingly tall wizard-like being, scampers forwards, stares at me, then at my weapon. It motions for a young companion to pick up the bow and arrow, they turn their backs, and the whole pack runs away into the distant marshes.

'Now we have no weapons,' Cai moans.

'That's how it is meant to be played. Pia is a non-violent eco-warrior. You just wait and see …'

Following the wylver, I search for gorse, fearing exposure on this wild plain. I dart from rock to rock, alert to possible future attacks. The secret of the whin? I need to locate Castle of Ceòlm. Is there a cliff, or a mound? Where would people want to defend themselves around here?

Then I remember. Last year Mum and Dad took us there. Cai was studying castles so they insisted he experienced a real-life fortified manor house. While they sat eating the picnic on the grassy promontory, not unlike Caernef, overlooking the sea, I wandered back to the castle. Exploring, as Miranda of course, I climbed the stone stairs, slipping under the *do-not-pass-this-point* notice, and I roamed the crumbling ruin. From the highest parapet, I could see bright gorse bushes below. I remember because I was looking out for a yellowhammer. I could hear its call, *a little bit of bread and no cheese,* but I couldn't see it.

It is possible Nathan and his programmers saw me there, replicating the scene. So, I run. Across the common to a group of agricultural buildings, past the stacked hay bales, up the track. I know the way. A stone fortress appears on the horizon. Not far. Accelerate up the track, checking behind, to the sides. No wylver here. I can even remember the location of the gorse bushes.

But there is a lure. A virtual decoy intended to divert me from the scent. Trumpet fanfare.

'Look! Poppy there's our clue; that eagle!'

'It's not an eagle, and I don't trust it. Let me see …' I zoom in, and my gut reaction is confirmed, 'It is a great skua. Not our friend, Cai. Leave it alone. Pirate of the seas.

It is a pillager. Kills puffin. I've never seen a real one.'

The skua persists in tempting us to follow it along the clifftop, but I resist, intent on locating the whin. I run round the castle walls, not pausing to peer round any corners. A sea mist lurks offshore, and the ancient ruined walls of the fortified manor house block my way. Not to be beaten, I climb, spotting the *do-not-pass-this-point* notice. Astounded by the precise details of my life that Nathan is able to capture and recreate, I clamber, surefooted, over the lower fortifications, and am rewarded. I catch sight of golden flowers shining through mounds of prickles.

'The whin. The gorse. Well done, Poppy!'

'But what now? Where is the secret?'

'In the bushes of course …'

I look down at my … Pia's … bare arms, wondering where her jacket is, or any gloves. 'It's no good diving straight in. I need protection, and we need more information about where in the whin.' The great skua is still circling on the horizon, taunting me. The damp sea breeze tickles my cheeks. Virtuality is truly incredible, but I need protection. I cast my mind back to the afternoon at the fortified manor house. Where did I leave my coat, and did I have gloves?

Without explaining to Cai, I take off, away from the whin, back over the crumbling walls towards the car park. But there is no car park. They have written it out of the scene. I stand, as Pia, at the junction of fiction and reality, trying to read the minds of the programmers. They have junked anything boring and enhanced the visuals. They have rewritten my life for an audience. Where is my coat?

I scan my surroundings, discerning a solitary figure far away on the plateau, but approaching at speed. Not a figure. A horse maybe? I lean against the stone wall, blending into the background, hiding and waiting. Pia's rhythmic breathing in my ears.

'Come on, Pops!'

'Shh; we must wait …'

Cai spots the approaching creature too, 'Oh it's only a wylver. They pop up all over the place. Ignore it. We have no weapons anyway.'

The grand old wylver crests the rise and plunges down towards the castle, seeking me. Silently, I step out on to the rough ground, to watch it approach. It notices me, raises a foreleg in recognition and, panting, crouches at my feet. Gathering its breath, the wylver smiles, a curious cracked-teeth smile. We can even smell its musty breath. Next, it removes its grey cloak, as well as the two protective gloves on its front hooves, revealing wizened skin. It places them before me, disappearing in a puff of sparkling smoke.

I grab the cloak, assuming that one good turn deserves another. After all, I spared its life. I throw the cloak over my shoulders, putting my tiny hands into the rough gauntlets. Expecting simple protection against the prickly bushes, I try to run back towards the whin, but my body is tingling, and my limbs are not my own. I know that I must make it to the whin. With a gargantuan effort, I drag my leaden feet towards the bushes and grab a spiny frond.

The moment I grip the prickly gorse with the wylver's glove on my hand, wrenching a piece off the bush, dramatic explosions of colour fill the screen to firework music. For an instant, my eyes are blinded and my ears deafened by the tumultuous cacophony. Immobile, I stand, waiting for the eruption to subside.

'Don't worry, that's virtuality. Players like a good celebration,' Cai reassures me.

As the dust settles, I find myself in an underground room, still wearing the wylver's cloak and gloves.

'Quick Poppy, you must put the whin in the machine. Quick!' Cai urges. I am still getting used to the ways of virtuality where reality and imagination merge in the moment, rising and falling in an uneasy harmony, to create an engaging game.

One of Nathan's programmers has designed a

convoluted metal locking system for this underground doorway. It doesn't take us long to work out that the spikey whin must be placed in a fireproof box, and lit from a handy candle. As the mechanism heats up, after some mechanical wizardry, the door opens, revealing a second door.

Pinned on this second door is a sign I recognise. It says, *Earthworks*.

'Damnation!'

'What?'

'*Earthworks*. I recognise it.' Cheated by Miranda, my blood boils. She was working with Nathan all along. She was just setting up some scenes for virtuality. She didn't need me to spy for her at all. All I manage is to mumble, 'Remind me, Cai, *never* to trust Miranda again.'

Suddenly exhausted by the effort of living through someone else's manifestation of me, I pass the controller back to Cai and say I need some fresh air. This isn't working.

....

Several days later, after college, when my brain is full with ecosystems and underpinning evidence, Cai calls me upstairs to his gaming station, squeezed up against the end of his bed. He motions for me to sit beside him. We are engulfed by the alluring soundtrack before I have even begun operating.

'I don't want to do any more Pia,' I blurt out, explaining, 'It's no good for me. I'm still too angry. I need to *do* something about it, Cai. I need to …'

'Quiet, big sister! Look here. Do you recognise any of these people?'

Curious, I peer at the screen. Around the underground Tarquin table sits a gathering of a dozen shadowy characters. Initially, I don't recognise any of them.

'Tarquin.'

'Tarquin?'

'That's where I was, with Miranda. The underground

board room is at Tarquin.'

Cai manipulates Pia's hand to type T-A-R-Q-U-I-N. A box on the table opens, revealing digital papers.

'Fantastic! Thanks Poppy.'

I glower and escape downstairs where Mum is chopping vegetables for tea.

'What's up Poppy?'

'Nothing.'

'Well, it must be something? You look like I feel some days. It's school again, isn't it?'

I have neglected Mum lately, and feeling guilty, give her a hug.

'What was that for, darling?'

'I don't like *you* to feel down, Mum.'

'Well, I have good reason. When they have reclaimed the deeds for the cottage, for *our home*, where will we go? Dad, you and Cai are too relaxed about it. It is a real possibility. We are completely helpless. There's no paperwork proving our right to live here. I've been homeless, Poppy, and I don't want that for you, or for Cai …'

'But Mum, Robin owns the cottage. She would never let anyone take it from us. Anyway, she needs us here to look after her.'

'But that land-grabbing *Executive Property* wants the clifftop and the cottage to expand their operations. Robin says it is all getting out of control. She was too trusting when the contract was drawn up, moreover, she needed the money. They are walking all over us.'

Mum turns towards me, anger bubbling just below the surface. I should be helping her to fight this, rather than dabbling in some ridiculous cybergame.

'Could you be a dear and take Dad his coffee? It's going cold. He is out harvesting beans. He should have come in by now.'

I would like to ask Dad about the cottage, so take the coffee and seek him out. It is the end of the bean crop this week; the autumn is arriving with the first frost on the horizon. There is a nip in the air as I wander along the doomed bean rows, already a few shrivelled carcasses dangling from the once voluptuous plants. I can hear Dad singing to himself. Some ancient Lebanese song from his childhood. The plants are trembling, giving away his location. I pop out from behind the beanstalks, and shout, 'Boo!'

Dad jumps, laughs and thanks me for his coffee, which he gulps down before resuming picking. I join him, snapping the remaining beans from their stalks.

'There's still loads on here. Worth coming out one last time,' he comments enthusiastically, 'but they will be a bit stringy. Beggars can't be choosers.'

I pick fast, launching each bundle of beans into his basket.

'Thanks Poppy.'

'Dad. Mum is worrying about the cottage. What exactly is Executive Property doing?'

'I know. Poor Maria. Always worrying about something these days, but she is right to be concerned. They are keen to absorb the cottage and the land around it into their existing plot. They are offering Robin some hefty sums but she won't agree. They want to expand into a theme-park-style holiday village. I've seen the plans. Hen parties, wedding venue, glamping. All that sort of thing. We can't stay if that happens. It would be sacrilege.'

But Caernef … Dad … the wildlife … the peace and quiet. It would all be ruined.'

'I know. Don't you worry about it, Poppy. It's bad enough having Mum moping around.'

'I will go and talk to Robin.'

'Good luck. Maybe she'll listen to you. Anyway, how's school? Is it good to be back?'

'The same as ever, and no: I don't want to be there, and I don't want to study boring science …'

We pick the final few beans in an awkward silence, so I

ask Dad whether he will be pulling the plants up tonight, but he says it is getting dark. Better to tackle that tomorrow. We load the baskets on our shoulders, stowing the beans into the vegetable store. Mum is going to prepare them for the freezers this evening. They wilt if they are left more than a couple of hours off the plant.

'I think I will pop down to see Robin before supper.' I actually want to avoid Cai calling me back to help out with Pia.

'Okay; see you later Love.'

....

Robin is in good spirits when I arrive, despite a huge plaster on her head and a bandaged ankle. She has received a real paper letter from her old friend Gid, announcing he is coming to visit, with his family. Last time Gid came, a couple of years ago, his twin boys were tiny babies. Robin's excitement is infectious. We share memories of Gid from the early days of Caernef, and forget our worries for a while.

'So, tell me about Pia, Poppy,' she asks, taking me aback.

'Oh, Pia … but I came to ask you about the threat to our home from Executive Property.'

'Those capitalists,' she retorts, 'I should never have entered into a deal with them.'

'We needed the money, Robin.'

'And we need it again, but not at the expense of the cottage, or the hillside around it. Never over my dead body.'

'Mum is really worried. I want to help.'

'Hm. There may be something you can do to help indirectly, which is why I was going to ask you about this Pia thing. Gid mentioned it in his letter. What do you know about this virtuality game of Nathan's, Poppy?'

I do trust Robin, of course I do, but I struggle to bring myself to talk about Pia. Where would I begin? She misinterprets my silence and brushes it off.

'Never mind dear. I just wondered if you could explain it to me. As you know, I have never played computer games. I only use the internet for campaigning, which is another thing I wanted to tell you about; #FutureProof is beginning to gain a great deal more support. Guess who from?'

I shake my head, still wrangling with my dilemma over Pia.

'The runners. You know, *my* runners.'

This is interesting. I adore the runners. They used to have huge meetings at Caernef. There were truly fascinating characters, who made such a fuss of me. Since they were nationalised, they have become boring and institutional. They have lost their spirit. Runners still come to visit, but it's nothing like it used to be. Even the earths, the off-grid communities, have fallen out with each other. The leaders seem to spend more time squabbling than focusing on their original vision for the future. A carbon-neutral planet, eco-living, equity and kindness. Earths and runners were the high point of my childhood.

'Tell me, Robin. I want to know.'

My enthusiasm fuels hers, and she relates her latest successes, which seem to have emanated from one of Miranda's meetings in Westminster. National politics is unstable once more, and there is a hint that the management of the runners is going to be outsourced. The old guard is asking Robin to become involved again.

....

Gid and his wife Juliette arrive late, on a Friday night at the end of October. It's half-term, and I'm desperate for a diversion from endless boring science homework. The twins, Arran and Marty, are asleep in the car, so we carry them into the dormitory we have hired from Executive Property for the weekend. The camp is closed for half-term cleaning as well as renovations, so, out of hours, we have the run of the place, just like the old days. Dad has lit the fire pit, and Uncle Glyn has brought crates of beer from The Prince of Wales. The sound of guitars lures Arran and Marty out from their bunks. I hold their little pudgy hands, while we dance by the light of the moon. Their eyes sparkle at the wonders of Caernef on a warm autumn night, reminding me of Cai at that age. Even Robin is the life and soul of the party. She hovers around Gid, grabbing conversation with him between the songs.

Mum, cheered up by this heart-warming gathering, produces a feast for us, and we are partying well into the night.

I haven't seen Uncle Glyn for months. We wander round the deserted parade ground, smiling at the bursts of song from the campfire, and he asks me about Pia, concern on his face.

'To tell the truth Uncle Glyn, I'm incandescent.'

'How has Nathan done it, Poppy? I mean, how could he?'

I show him the tiny area of raised skin in my arm, and explain how I believe I have been digitally tracked, for most of my life. Glyn has always been mild-mannered. I have never heard him angry, but something hits a raw nerve with him.

'That is fucking abuse Poppy. Excuse me swearing. How could he do this to you? You are *the* original child of Caernef. We all love you, want to protect you. You grew up with us as your extended family. It was unspoken that each one of us would always protect you. Not this. Not exploitation of the worst kind. I thought Nathan was my friend, until I heard of this. What are you going to do about it?'

While I consider his question, relieved to be talking openly about Pia, with someone who is so unequivocally on my side, an owl shrieks above our heads.

'It's a good omen, a little owl,' Glyn observes, and we just catch sight of the beautiful bird as the firelight plays on the branches. 'So, what shall we do about it, Poppy? You're not on your own with this.'

For the first time since I discovered my virtual alter-ego, I feel protected. We wander back to the fireside together, to discover Gid and Robin making an announcement.

'So tomorrow morning, we will sign on the dotted line,' Robin is declaring, with unusual glee.

'Here's to the future!' Dad raises his tankard. Everyone is cheering and chattering with enthusiasm.

'Hold on now; what have we missed?' Glyn demands.

As the revellers calm, and the crackle of the wood on the fire can be heard, Gid explains, his huge powerful body rising up as a silhouette behind the flames, 'Nathan is back on board. Not only that, but he is prepared to fund our bid to manage the runners again …'

'Nathan?' Uncle Glyn blurts out, exchanging a look with me.

'Yes, isn't that amazing,' chimes in Robin, 'Gid has organised it all. At last, we will be back together again; the original gang. Miranda too.'

Cai slides beside me on the bench, and whispers, 'Don't panic, Poppy. It will all work out.'

7: Reunion

In virtuality, the first reunion of Robin's original team was masterminded by Nathan, in the basement at Tarquin, accompanied by full orchestra. His programmers sculpted barely recognisable recreations of Robin, Gid, Nathan, Eva and Miranda; Robin's random companions, who escaped the glitch together. The original gang walked hundreds of miles to Caernef at the time of the terrible glitches. They joined Mum and Dad here, when I was only three years old, over a decade ago. In reality, and quite appropriately, their *actual* reunion is being held at Caernef.

Nathan has flown in by techno-copter and is totally ignoring me. Cai was fascinated by the state-of-the-art transport. Even Miranda has turned up, only slightly late, artificially gushing, so I totally ignored her. I was happiest to see Robin's old friend Eva, still beaming cheerfully through her rainbow colours. She arrived with gifts for everyone, including a notebook with a celestial design on the cover, for me, filled with handmade paper from an earth.

Mum, Dad, Uncle Glyn, Cai and I are not included in the first part of the meeting, so we are sitting out the back of the cottage, overlooking the allotments and the chicken run, on the slope down towards the sea, reminiscing while we wait. I am gazing mindlessly at *Physics Experimentation.* Gid is going to call us when they are ready. His partner, Juliette, has taken the twins off for a walk on the foreshore, as they are not included either.

'I haven't seen Robin look as well as this for years,' Mum comments, while she refills cups of tea. She is right. Robin is rejuvenated and purposeful. I wonder whether they will let Cai and I join in with them this time. After all, we are old enough to understand fully now.

'There's something about in the offing about Executive Property,' Uncle Glyn mutters. I move to sit next to him on the picnic bench.

'What do you know, Uncle Glyn?'

'I *don't* know. That's the frustration, but Nathan is involved. I overheard him tell Robin the EP contracts are signed and they are ready to go.'

Dad is earwigging, 'I bet they are inviting a rep from EP to join them in managing the runners. That's the last thing we need …'

I whisper to Cai, 'Robin will be trying to save the cottage for us, I know it.' Cai squeezes my hand, raising his eyebrows in a hopeful but silent gesture.

…………

It is Eva who reappears to call us over. She is all smiles, and ushers us into the dormitory at the front of the parade ground; the one overlooking the estuary. We file in, uncertainly. I am nervous, intent on keeping my anger with Nathan, and with Miranda, my dubious heroine, under wraps.

The usual furniture has been cleared back, with the large circular table set up at the front, overlooking the view. Robin, with her back to the estuary, organises seating, inviting Cai and I to take the two wooden storyteller chairs in prime position at the head of the table. I was not expecting such prominence.

We don't need introductions, so Robin dives straight in, 'We are gathered here on this momentous occasion to put the world back on its axis,' continuing, 'It is ironic it was the terrible glitch that fortuitously brought us together all those years ago. Since that time, we set up Caernef as an alternative way of living, close to nature, outside the constraints of capitalism. We created the runners, mobilised the earths through #isolate. We triumphed in national politics, with #Spoiler.' She stares thoughtfully at the faces round the table, one by one, adding, 'But then, we went our separate ways.'

Robin pauses for effect. I study the circle of expectant conspirators, waiting for something big; something momentous …

'Friends, this is the time for us to rise again. Not for our own aggrandisement, not for profit or even by stealth, but openly and honestly for the future of the planet. We are *called.* We are *needed.* From our unique position outside the mainstream, here at Caernef, we can act. Our world is in severe difficulty, and we need to act *now.*'

She pauses again, and I expect Miranda to intervene, or Mr High and Mighty Nathan to take over, but their respect for Robin is intense, despite her poor health, her wrinkles and her oddities.

'First of all, we must remember our original pledge, which still holds us together. Through *equity and innovation*, the values of the runners, we are all equal, no matter how young, or how old, whether we are rich or poor, feeble or … as strong as Gid!'

Gid grins with embarrassment, but each member of the assembled company is looking serious.

'And we are committed to innovation,' Robin continues, 'to find new ways of doing things, not bound by the idiocies of the past.' For an instant she flounders, unsure, but she gathers herself, announcing a new value to bind us together, that of *honesty.* She looks directly at Miranda while she speaks, and Miranda, ever-confident, returns the stare, unwavering. I try to catch Nathan's eye, but he is studiously avoiding any contact with me.

'There are several matters to clear up before we begin on the real business,' Robin explains. She invites Nathan to tell us all about Executive Property. Mum and Dad sit up straight in their chairs, eager but fearful.

Nathan has never been the most confident of speakers, but he has always commanded respect for his ingenuity. As I listen to him speak, I feel demeaned. I feel suspicious. I am totally overwhelmed with a sadness, which I cannot explain. This young man, for all his bravado, has exploited me. I consider leaving the meeting, but I cannot. I hold my ground and cling to the sides of the chair. It is too important.

'Virtuality took off more than I imagined,' Nathan begins. 'I never set out to make money. I have been waiting for the right opportunity to get back in touch with Robin … with you guys.'

Robin leans over, patting his arm in encouragement, which disgusts me. Can't she see through his veneer of false loyalty?

'Anyway,' he continues, 'first thing is, I've signed an agreement with our friends at Executive Property.'

I catch Dad's eye, as he gulps. This will mean the difference between staying or leaving Caernef. Mum cannot help herself, 'Well Nathan, what is it? What have you come all this way to tell us?'

Nathan remains unflustered, seeming to enjoy making us wait. The prerogative of the wealthy.

'I have settled the break clause and they will cut all ties with Caernef from Monday. The thing is, virtuality will definitely be a hands-off management company. I … we … will need you one hundred percent on board. Caernef will have to be run as it used to be, but this time, at a profit. No bailing out.'

'And the cottage?' Cai bursts out.

Nathan smiles beneficently, 'I know you have had a hell of a worry about things, but the lease is being drawn up as we speak. Robin is in charge of it and will work with you. It will be a protected lifetime tenancy, on a peppercorn rent. It will run for the lifetime of all current residents. That was the best I could organise in the time. We can talk it through later. I just wanted you to know.'

After a short silence, while this news sinks in, Mum, Dad, and Cai all launch themselves on Nathan, followed by everyone else, except me. They hug him, they cheer, they act like they have won the Lottery. I am both embarrassed, as well as flabbergasted, that they can so quickly forget about Pia, and my dilemma.

No one seems to notice my reticence, although Uncle Glyn comes over and high-fives with me, winking, I think he wants to help me cover up my desperation.

As the dormitory settles down, Nathan has clearly become the Prodigal Son, and instead of all turning to Robin, they all turn to him, expecting more. They are not disappointed.

'Anyway, let's move on from domestic matters, to our bid for the coordination of the earths and the runners,' Nathan looks to Robin to give him the floor. She nods, having lost her usual tense look, so Nathan continues. 'Miranda has organised the writing of the bid, as she has contacts in The Department. Virtuality is backing it. That is, *virtuality*, not me personally. I have the agreement of shareholders and trustees. If we are successful, we are back in business.'

'When will we know?' Gid demands.

'They are keen to fast-track this one, and as bidding closed a couple of weeks ago, we could be awarded the contract any day. We should have called a meeting earlier.'

'So, who is named in the bid. We didn't know anything about it. What if we don't agree,' Uncle Glyn seems to be covering my back. I was thinking exactly that, but didn't have the courage to ask.

'It is a generic bid. It only names Caernef Enterprises, which doesn't fully exist yet. It is a dormant company, while we organise ourselves. Anyone who wants to be involved can be voted on to the board today. We've got to act fast.'

After a lengthy discussion about the practicalities of

coordinating the runners again, Robin turns towards Cai and I, explaining slowly and calmly why we are to be invited to join the adults. 'You see, we are all getting older. Many of the runners are a third of my age now. We need you two to represent young people. Poppy, you first. It is no coincidence we have hung on as long as possible, so that you are old enough, as we are establishing an incorporated charity, you can join. Cai, you can shadow Poppy, and we will officially co-opt you in a few years' time. We absolutely need you two involved and committed. In fact, we cannot proceed unless you are in agreement.'

Robin had the conversation with Mum and Dad earlier this morning, but this comes out of the blue for me and Cai. I look around the room. Who do I trust to give me the advice I need right now? I trust Eva, but she is too nice. I need someone tough. I trust Uncle Glyn, but he is too laid back. Mum, Dad and Cai are partisan. They are all pressuring me, gabbling on about me being *the child of Caernef*. They are so pleased for me, expecting me to jump at the opportunity.

'How about we break for a drink?' I attempt. Mum, of all people, rescues me, saying she has cake and Caernef produce to hand round. Robin announces a break of twenty minutes.

....

Avoiding Nathan, I exit quickly, gather all the resolve I can, and corner Miranda. She is on her phone. I wait so close to her that she cannot ignore me. As soon as she cuts the call, I goad, 'Bet I can reach the flagpole quicker than you.' She runs. I run. I am not being her. I am not being Pia. I am being myself, standing up for myself, and staking my claim to her time. At last.

We leave the others chatting, and sprint the hundred yards up the field and across the parade ground. I am used to the terrain, so I inch ahead. She isn't wearing the right footwear for speed, but in my boots, I grip the soil, surging forwards. She finds some strength at the last, touching the flagpole a millisecond before me, as we tumble in a heap on the mud, laughing. That is how it used to be, before she left and became important.

'You win Miranda!'

'You're quick Poppy. Next time …'

I am not even panting, whereas she is gasping for breath, brushing herself down. My trick has worked. I just need to keep her attention. I slip my hand into my pocket and grip Arcadian B. 'What has it got in its pocketses?' I ask with a wry smile. We used to play games like this when I was tiny. She remembers.

Miranda closes her eyes, asking, 'How many guesses?'

'Three.'

'An oke.'

'No.'

'A feather?'

'No.' She looks into my eyes, as if extracting my thoughts. I will her to guess, as then she will be triumphant, and well-disposed towards me. 'It binds us together,' I hint.

'Arcadian B. Of course!'

I reveal the tiny silver bee, Nathan's prototype, which he has probably forgotten, but Miranda hasn't.

Her phone rings. For the first time ever, I hear her say, 'It can wait.' She continues, 'So, Poppy, you wanted to ask me something. You didn't want to ask Robin, or your family, or the others. You wanted to ask me. Spit it out.'

The real Miranda. My Miranda.

'I need your help.'

'Right …?'

'Miranda, I will only join this new thing of theirs IF Nathan takes down Pia. Pia I, Pia II and any future plans he has. I want you to back me. They will listen to you.'

'Hmmm.'

'I will refuse to join, if Pia remains there between us.' I glare into her eyes to emphasize my point. 'It would be a shame for a silly computer game to stand in the way of us saving the world.'

Miranda teases me for being too serious about Pia, and I begin to lose hope. Her phone rings again. She grips the phone, suddenly hurling it high into the air, way over the edge of the parade ground, to clatter down on the rocks. We listen to the crack as it lands. But she doesn't go after it.

'I did that once before, Poppy, on to the railway track. This place gets to you, doesn't it?' It is rhetorical. 'I will back you; I promise. I wouldn't want to have had my private existence exposed for the cyber masses to drool over either. Let's return to the others. We must press on. Lots to cover today in very little time.'

Do I believe her?

....

Back round the grand wooden table, the dust in the dormitory catching the sunlight, Cai and I sit on our thrones. They talk through what will be needed for the runner's contract, if we win it. We plan how Caernef Camp will be managed, without the devilish partner Executive Property and its various arms-length subcontracts. Uncle Glyn, who has been retired for some time, is very keen to come back to manage the site with Dad, and eventually this is agreed. The two old friends shake hands, slapping each other on the back, clearly delighted at this prospect.

As they move on to establishing the new management board, to oversee both enterprises, Miranda looks at me and winks. She intervenes in her dramatic style.

'To be honest, we can't do any of this unless Poppy is in agreement. We Know we need the younger generation on board; it's central to our plan for the success of #FutureProof.'

This is the first mention of #FutureProof.

Each one of them, except Nathan, turns to look at me. Silence. Expectation. Miranda, not known for her patience, gives me a prompt, 'Speak up, Poppy.'

So, I speak up. I rise from my seat, slowly gaining eye contact round the room, forcing Nathan to turn his petrified hazel eyes on me once again, after all these years. I try to use Robin's visionary eloquence and Miranda's directness. I get straight to the point, 'I'm sorry, friends; although I sign up to your ideals, although I welcome the return of Caernef to our control, and I would love to become more involved in supporting the runners, I cannot join you.'

Pleased with my contribution, I sit down, dramatically, surprised that when I needed the right words to come out of my mouth, for once, they came.

Robin speaks up, breaking the stunned silence, 'Why not, Poppy, dear? You must explain …'

'I grew up here at Caernef trusting you all. I was fortunate to have had such a special childhood, but I am not a child any more. I will take back control of my own life …' I couldn't say it.

'Spit it out Poppy,' Miranda intervenes. I really don't want her to have to explain, so I try again.

'My very existence has been violated in virtuality. Nathan, if you do not close down Pia. I mean Pia I, Pia II and any other iterations of Pia. If you don't stop violating me in this way, then I am sorry, but I will have to decline my involvement in anything further here at Caernef.'

Mum leans across to calm me down, but I shrug her off, and instead, I say it again, just to make sure Nathan has been listening, 'Pia must end, Nathan. I never consented, and you know it.'

For the second time this decade, at Caernef, Nathan is in the firing line. He drops his gaze and shakes his head.

The wailing cries of gulls break into the awkward silence. My friends are looking down at the table, and out of the window. Divided loyalties.

Robin makes a decision, ending the embarrassed confusion, 'Friends, we will have to take another short break. I would like to meet with Nathan and with you,

Poppy, at the folly. Let's talk this through.'

Nathan nods and I say clearly, 'Okay with me.'

…………

Shaking off the hugs and kind words, I walk resolutely towards the folly, alone. But just before I reach the door, Nathan appears. He corners me on the doorstep, and without giving me a chance to escape, or to protest, he splutters, 'Poppy, I am sorry. I'm really sorry. It got out of hand. I should have spoken with you before, I know that. Can we talk? Please?'

'Okay …'

Robin arrives, panting from the short walk, and sits on the bench to rest her legs.

'Can you give Nathan and I a few minutes Robin?'

'Of course. I'm here when you are ready. We need to resolve this; you both know that, and we don't have time on our side.'

Nathan's apparent contrition has somehow dissipated my anger. He looks distraught. This is unexpected. I suggest, quietly, 'Shall we walk down to the arcade?'

'The arcade?'

'Your old workshop; you know?'

'Yes.'

Nathan follows me, as I gaze silently out at the estuary. The unforgettable Caernef magic is seeming to work further on his conscience.'

'I really am sorry Poppy. Seeing you in the flesh, so grown up, so in control of yourself. It brings it home to me.'

We reach the arcade. Nathan hesitates as I unlock, both of us breathing deeply. He walks inside, gasping at the real-life beauty of my Caernef treasures, arranged around the debris of his cyberjunk.

'It smells the same,' he mutters. Virtuality didn't capture that.'

'Nathan, I want you to stop this Pia nonsense. Please Nathan.'

'Pia is my life, Poppy. You don't understand. Pia is the most sublime creation, which is why all the punters love her. She is addictive. Pia is pure; she is all the things most people have lost. She smells of wild thyme in the sun on the Caernef clifftop, she is wreathed in exquisite music. Pia is massively successful. I have saved every penny generated from her directly, to put into this new Caernef project. The royalties set aside for you have been taken from the general virtuality fund. You will be able to access them; they will be life-changing for you. Robin couldn't be doing this without the income from Pia. It is Pia who has saved the cottage for your family …'

Perhaps ungratefully, I burst out, 'Cut the crap Nathan. I want Pia to be terminated. It is necessary for our next steps at Caernef. Robin needs me on board. Pia is the problem. She must go.'

Nathan perches on my stool, which was once his stool, and he sighs. 'It's not as simple as you make it sound.' Then, moving to the back of the arcade, he raises the oilcloth and asks for a screwdriver. Fortunately, I keep a box of tools down here, scavenged from the mess he left behind. I produce one, he clambers awkwardly under the platform, unscrews a cover, and hands me the precious screws to hold. Like he used to do. He fiddles with the switches and wires hidden underneath.

Four miniscule screws; the key to my freedom.

'That's the transponder disconnected. I can organise for your micro-implant to be removed. I don't want to do it myself. It needs to be done properly, especially after so long.'

'Thank you. And Pia?'

'Pia is everywhere. Pia I and Pia II have been amazing successes. I can't just end it. Besides …'

'Besides?'

'Don't take this the wrong way, but I love Pia. She has become a part of my life, which I cannot give up.'

I guessed as much, beginning to feel uncomfortable.

'Hey Poppy, hand me the screws and I will put this cover back on.'

Suddenly it is like when I was tiny, and I helped Nathan with his projects. As I hand him the screws, our fingers touch, but I am nervous.

'We need to go back to Robin.'

Without speaking, Nathan stands up, sending a cloud of dust into the air. He looks around the arcade. My arcade.

'Did you see the sea eagle, Nathan?'

'I saw the sea eagle through your geotracker Poppy. I have seen this workshop day after day, but now I am actually here; here with you, virtuality seems so …'

'Unreal?'

'No. Unimportant. Come on Poppy, let's sort this out with Robin. I think we both want the same outcome; the challenge will be how to get there.'

This time, Nathan leads the way. I watch his back as he strides purposefully towards the folly. I'm not going to give up on this. It is my one chance to get my own life back. Trouble is, it is actually too late. As he says, Pia is out there, indelibly imprinted. I will never be able to escape.

Robin is waiting for us. She wants to get back to the others so we can all move forwards. Nathan is fiddling nervously with his phone. He and Robin have patched up their big falling out of ten years ago, but the atmosphere is uneasy. She starts by appealing to me, 'Poppy, we can't do this without Nathan. Much as I despise accumulated wealth, we need the Pia fund to get Caernef back on track. We need to be back in charge, and to bid for the runners. Pia will enable us to do that. You can enable us to do that.'

'It's alright Robin, we are ahead of you. I understand. All I am saying is that from this day, there is no more Pia. Kill her off or something.'

Nathan winces, snapping, 'I can't just kill her off.'

Robin appeals to us both, 'Maybe you should work on Pia's future together. Poppy understands her character.

Nathan, you have the tech. Write a future for Pia *together*. Make her the ultimate eco-hero. Make Pia the new Robin …’

8: Rio

It is dark by the time I manage to creep away from the reunion. The enthusiastic members of the Caernef crowd are sharing memories and planning the future, squashed into the lounge at home, beside a roaring fire. It is the first of the season, and their faces are glowing, also, no doubt, due to the hearty supper, and a rather strong *fruit* punch. I hope I will not be missed, as I have an important task to perform.

Fortunately, the moon is bright tonight, so I can easily find my way down towards the edge of the cliff. Trying to recall the exact spot, I scan the rocks below the parade ground, but I can't see it. Maybe she came back for it. Maybe a seabird fancied it and sent it tumbling down the cliff into the waves.

On the verge of giving up, I spot a shard catching the moonlight. Standing still, holding my breath, it continues to wink at me from a crevice, at the back of an awkward shelf of rock. Might be something else. Deciding that it is worth pursuing, I stretch my leg down on to the scree, perform a little jump, steady myself, and clamber towards the location. Should have brought a stronger torch, but I fumble into the crevice where I think I saw it, and my fingers close on the familiar smooth surface of a mobile phone. Not any mobile phone, but Miranda's.

Robin has urged us to be honest, but I feel I must do this. Dishonesty, after all, is Miranda's business. It is too tempting; I manage to retrieve the phone, easing my way slowly back on to the top of the cliff. I scamper to the arcade, cradling my booty, relieved to see that although the screen has one large crack across it, the phone is intact. I stow it under Nathan's now deactivated platform.

Caught unawares, I jump at the sound of footfall outside. and freeze to the spot as I hear a raucous hammering on the door of the arcade. Please, please let it not be Nathan.

Cai bounds in, 'We were wondering where you were. I thought I'd find you down here.'

Cai, it's good to see you. I'm coming home now. Let's go together,' I grin with relief.

While we walk, Cai asks me about Nathan, kindly. I do not mention Miranda's phone, but I do tell him about the platform being disabled, and that I demanded the end of Pia.

'Oh, but she is *so* good,' he whines.

'That's what Nathan said. In fact, I think Nathan is in love with Pia.'

'But she isn't real?'

'*I* know that, but she is real to *him*,' I state, resolutely, adding, 'There are plenty of people out there in love with avatars.'

Cai changes the subject. 'Anyway, it's fantastic news about home being saved. Mum and Dad are made up. Haven't seen Mum so cheerful for ages.'

'Yes. I never thought I'd see the whole crowd back together here. It's magic.'

'And the runners, Poppy, … they are planning a big event, like when we were little.'

I have so many memories. 'I collected the empty bottles. Miranda was outside the fence at that time.'

'I don't remember much. I was too young, but I've seen the footage.'

Recalling one of my childhood jingles, I start to sing, *We are going to stoptheglitch, stoptheglitch, stoptheglitch; we are going to stoptheglitch early in the morning.*

'But it's FutureProof now …' Cai retorts.

…………

Every time I come into the arcade, checking Miranda's phone is still there, I mean to do it, but I haven't the courage. The phone is out of charge and the screen is fragile from the impact on the rocks. But my mind is on my arm. This time I have brought a sterilised scalpel, as well as disinfectant wipes, so I can't chicken out. There's no way I am telling Mum about it, and Cai is the only person who knows, apart from Nathan of course. Nathan is so busy he has forgotten that he said he could organise for it to be removed. I have decided I have to just do it myself, but I am frightened.

Wonder whether I can remove it without having to look too hard at it. It's fairly near the surface; I can feel the bump.

Hell, I can't do this. I take a walk out on to the headland, free from the burden that Nathan and his tech cronies are following my every move. That is, if he *really* disabled the system. Which I think he did.

Take a deep breath. Focus. I test the blade of the scalpel against my skin. It's damn sharp. Suddenly, and a tad clumsily, I surprise myself. The small geotracker pops out easily, rolling on to the earth floor. Chiding myself for not achieving this long ago, I slap a disinfectant wipe on the tiny slice in my arm, feeling nothing. Breathe deeply. Amazed at my own strength of will. I smile to myself and sit down on the stool. A bit wobbly from fear, but no harm seems to have been done. Blood oozes from the wound, seeping through the wipe. I am prepared for this, so once I am sure the area is clean and dry, I apply a large adhesive dressing. I stuff the rubbish into my pocket, and stoop to retrieve the geotracker. Despite its miniscule size, it is disproportionately heavy, like a small bullet. It has travelled with me for ten years. Bizarre.

With determination, I march out on to the clifftop,

survey the scene. Mustering all my strength, I throw Nathan's tiny tracker right over the rocks, towards the water. But it dances down the scree and rests on the pebbles above the tideline, teasing me. Like Miranda's phone, it lies there for anyone to find.

With the top of my left arm beginning to throb, and with bright red blood seeping through the dressing underneath my thick sleeve, I hurry down the narrow path to the shoreline. Ecstatic that I have achieved my aim to remove the thing, I am lightheaded; anything seems possible now. Why on earth didn't I pluck up the courage earlier in my life? Keeping the exact location of the tracker in my mind, I balance across the rocks, scanning until I locate it, nestled innocently in a shallow rock pool, left marooned by the retreating tide. I bend, flicking it up into my hand, and walk to the water's edge, listening to the roar of the angry surf. Raising my good arm, I throw the damnable thing as far as I possibly can. A neat plop in the churning water, and it is gone.

Sorry Pia, but that's us divorced forever, I think to myself, as I heave a sigh of relief. I plant myself down on a boulder, listening to a faint but familiar noise; tat, tat, tat. At first, I think it is a robin, but then I realise that a solitary stonechat is pecking for seeds. Despite noticing me, it continues, scurrying towards me in fits and starts. When it is only a foot away, it pauses, then sings for a full two minutes, before flying off, back to the cover of the gorse at the foot of the cliff.

Comfort just when I needed it. Thank you, stonechat. I pick myself up, striding back along the path, check the arcade is clear of any debris, and head for home, in case my arm should flare up. Not sure what I would do if it did, but being near people would certainly be an advantage. Anyway, I have loads of homework to finish.

....

Nathan has, indeed, forgotten about the geotracker in Poppy's arm. He is more focused on Pia than Poppy.

In the three months since the autumn reunion, there have been changes at the bustling London headquarters of virtuality. Nathan still embodies the dynamic and purposeful leader, but for the new year, he relocated, with his top team, to the penthouse, previously occupied by a tech spin-off that lost its contract. Alongside the recently signed agreement with Caernef Enterprises, his team is working on the *new inspiration*, a cyber game rooted in #FutureProof, designed to propel Pia into a campaigning role.

'Tell me as soon as she arrives,' Nathan instructs Handsome, tidying his desk and scanning the minimalist office space to check nothing is out of place.

'She's not due for half an hour, Boss.' Handsome detects something beyond nerves in Nathan's demeanour. 'Try to chill,' he urges.

'I don't want any fuss. She says she isn't a celebrity. We need her one hundred percent onside. Don't want to scare her. She's used to the Welsh clifftop. I'm ging to put Rio in charge of her.'

'Of course. I know; remember? Don't fret!'

'Miranda Brenton is coming with her.'

'Don't I recognise that name from somewhere?'

'I bet you remember her when you see her.'

'Oh?'

'Miranda is … stunning … wicked … confusing. Anyway, she is in charge of the Oxford end of #Futureproof. Dances with diplomats and dodgy oligarchs'

'I see.' Handsome flicks dust from his desk, runs his fingers through his hair, straightens his jacket and brushes down his jeans. Nathan paces the room, and glances out of the window, comparing the rooftop views of London's Cyber City with the cliffs of Caernef. Some synergies, he thinks. But opposite. Totally opposite. Like Robin and Miranda. Both have a place. More pacing up and down.

'This is a risky strategy,' Handsome offers.

'Indeed. But the choice facing us is to terminate Pia, and abandon Pia III.'

'Impossible.'

'I know.'

....

It has been a frenetic few months, mostly due to the work needed at the camp to bring it back under our own management, as well, of course as the huge weight of four cumbersome sciences on my shoulders. There was no question of working at Tarquin over Christmas, my skills as cleaner, catering assistant and general dogsbody were needed at Caernef. It's been good fun working for Uncle Glyn, and I have always enjoyed mingling with the visitors, especially the runners, although the contract with the government is quite tight. We aren't allowed to be political this time, which hasn't gone down well with Robin, but we get round it.

There have been conferences, awaydays, meetings and, of course, the regular school visits.

As for Pia, that is the purpose of my visit today, with Miranda, to *virtuality*. I have never been there before. Nathan is being more accommodating and less demanding than I expected. Pia II and III are paused pending today's kickstart.

I refused to go alone, besides, Miranda, surprisingly, agreed to accompany me. Since I arrived in her office earlier, she has given me five-star treatment, and we have been driven to a well-to-do private mansion in central London, which Miranda calls *her club*. We have eaten lunch, and freshened up, before being driven to Cyber City, where virtuality is based. Prime location, Miranda says, close enough to the buzzing heart of London, but also near green spaces.

I was expecting London to be an exciting diversion from home, but it is cold, filthy, and too technological for its own good. Cyber City is the most extreme place I have ever been. Robin would hate it. As we drive up the boulevard, the skyscrapers clutter what must have been Essex marshes in a supposedly *tasteful* chaotic silver pile of random and ostentatious design. We weave through streets, which are totally in shade due to the huge buildings. 'These are all halls of residence for homeworkers,' Miranda explains. Graffiti, takeaway food and empty cycle racks. Up to the grand entrance of virtuality, where scurrying people carrying coffees are glancing up at Nathan's face displayed on an enormous screen, alongside several action shots of Pia.

Nervous, I stay close to Miranda, as we check in at the showy reception desk before being ushered into a lift. Miranda presses a gold button for the penthouse suite. She has been here before. I have never liked lifts, but I grit my teeth pretending it is fine, as we sail upwards towards Nathan.

'Hi, I'm Handsome.' A huge guy in a tight suit greets us at the very top of the building where even the doorhandles are digital. He escorts us to Nathan's private offices, staring at me the whole time. 'You're even more captivating in real life,' he volunteers. I am flustered. Don't know what to say. But it's no worry as we are propelled into Nathan's overheated office. He rises from his desk, surrounded by expansive screens, thanks Handsome, and welcomes us. Miranda seems at home here. She launches into a long discussion with Nathan about Cyber City, start-ups and talent pools, while I stand silently, taking it all in.

From the arcade in Caernef to the penthouse suite at Cyber City. Nathan has some story to tell.

He attempts to put me at my ease, offers me a chair at a computer, and switches to the end of Pia I, which plays over and over again. I am angry and hopeful simultaneously. Miranda draws up a chair on wheels, while Nathan leans over my shoulder, pointing out how the design controls work. Wish I brought Cai with me. He would know what to do.

'Nathan, have you set up Rio to work with Poppy?'

Miranda asks.

'Yep. It's all arranged.'

'I'd love to see Rio again.'

Miranda seems to know Rio, whoever he is.

I fumble with the controls, save my edit in the practice screen, waiting with anticipation.

Rio is a woman! I like her from the off. She has a kind face and quiet confidence. After Miranda has hugged her enthusiastically, Rio turns to me, 'Hi Poppy, I've been dying to meet you. Feel I know you already, as I was involved in the original character design. Nathan says we are going to work on the relaunch together. I'm so looking forward to it …'

....

That was the beginning of an intense week, working with Rio from dawn to dusk, sleeping in the posh virtuality visitor accommodation. Eating fast food. I haven't seen either Nathan, or Miranda, but they are returning today to view our work. It's daunting, although Rio has everything calmly in hand. We have mock-ups of the rewrite of the ending to Pia II, leading into Pia III. Spending so much dedicated time working on Pia has helped me to separate from her. She exists in her own right, and I am in control. This time.

Nathan appears with Handsome, coffees and bagels. No sign of Miranda. The four of us crowd round the designing screen. I wish Cai could see this. Rio demonstrates the character tweaks, an older Pia with a more mature look. She flashes through endless screens for them to approve the new designs; the recreation of Pia as an emerging campaigner and political force. Pia has slowly become more confident, less of a loner, plugged into the essential concerns of society: the future of the planet, investment in our ecosystems, and above all, the mobilisation of like-minded campaigners.

Having established a massive customer base, Nathan can now weave in the messages that he, and I, so want to push out there.

'When will it launch?' I ask.

Handsome and Rio look at Nathan. He consults the pocket computer he carries everywhere with him, scrolls, thinks, and decides, 'We will release the new extended ending for Pia II as soon as it is ready. No need to delay. Say four weeks. The fans will lap it up. Then build the anticipation for Pia III. Around … February 20th, ready for a half-term bonanza. That gives us a month to build momentum before we call the runners back to Caernef.'

He makes it sound so simple, until … 'I'll have to run it by the board, and once we have sign-off, I'll need to check it out with Miranda … oh and Robin, though she's not going to want this delayed. She has her plans for #FutureProof all in place already.'

So that's what Robin has been working on so quietly in the folly. I had wondered.

Nathan adds, 'Poppy, I will keep you updated on progress, but just assume it is all happening as we agreed. I will get the previews across to Cai so you can watch them together. You must let me know if at any time you are uncomfortable about anything.'

Once Nathan and Handsome have left, well-pleased with our work, Rio and I give each other modest gifts. I had a sumptuous scarf in my backpack, which I have never worn, made by a Welsh weaver. This delights her. In return, she hands me a package the size of a matchbox, wrapped in tissue paper. I peel off the paper to reveal the most amazing miniature hologram of Pia. 'They had it made early on, as a one-off, and I admired it in Nathan's basket of finds. He said I could keep it, but I want you to have it Poppy, to remember our work on the amazing ending of Pia II.'

Sad to leave my new-found friend, Miranda's transport arrives carrying me away, alone, towards Caernef. Me and my rucksack. Poppy Kiwan. Not Pia. Not at all.'

…………

Cai and I are playing in virtuality again. Nathan sends us new scenes each day, and we carve out time after college. I'm not getting down to the arcade as much as I would like, but we must get Pia right before the relaunch. She is, as Cai says, *supreme*. The work Rio and I sweated over has changed her from a naïve and alluring youngster, to a canny and determined teenager. Gameplayers will revel in the challenges we have set for her; leading her virtual followers into battle against the exploitative executives who covet material affluence. Not physical battles, of course, but battles of wit and determination. Pia and her gang succeed in establishing an outdoor ethical college. They secretly build the advanced ecotechnology, which is Nathan's forté, and they are about to conquer world markets from their clifftop, ready for Pia III.

Cai loves it. The gameplayers will love it. Pia is a clarion for change. She stands up for all that is simple, sustainable and collaborative, but is also worldly wise. A clever balance. The irony is explicit that it is a digital heroine who is the loudest critic of toxic dependence on digital leisure. What a point to be making! Because I am shaping this new Pia, I am becoming less angry, more at peace. There are elements of me in her, but she has risen as Pia in her own right, and she has an important job to do in championing #FutureProof.

....

In late March, Robin calls the runners back to Caernef, for the first time in years. We have succeeded in hiding the rendezvous below the radar of the press. Nathan has used virtuality staff to update all the old runner message encryptions using #isolate, and we are working through key contacts followed by word of mouth, in the old way through the earths, through the off-grid rural communities and urban networks. As Robin says, 'keeping things quiet is not a political act in itself …' We are working to a contract this time, and must be mega careful.

#isolate, I can see now, is a wry joke. I remember how

Robin used to say *isolate from society, isolate from the power games, which use loaded dice, isolate with people who you can trust. Hide and thrive. Protect and survive.* Her mantra became a song to me, as I ran the paths of Caernef, filled with inexplicable and half-understood optimism that the planet would be safe because of #isolate. But with the insight of age, and with the burden of Pia on my shoulders, I know #isolate is heavily ironic. It is not enough to isolate ourselves from the dominant culture strangling the planet, we have to somehow flip it over, and isolate the greed. If we are to rescue nature, we must isolate selfishness. #Futureproof is the way forwards. That's my mantra now.

Executive Property has finally removed its kit, taken down the sign boards, and vacated our precious headland. Cai and I had a party with fizzy pop and sweets from The Prince of Wales, a rarity for us, reminiscent of our younger days.

When I cleared the final piles of rubbish for incineration in the quarry, I discovered some glossy mock-ups of their advertising brochure for Caernef stag and hen parties. Good riddance to Executive Property.

Robin says the time is right. All her old followers agree, even Miranda. I am caught up in the momentum. Obsessed with the new Pia. Getting our messages out there.

9: Fingerprint

Several thousand keen runners of all ages surge forwards, along with representatives from the many earths across the country, as the band members stride out on to the clifftop stage, to open the event. Angelina is preparing to play lead guitar. She tunes up, strident in the spotlights, and tickles the strings to impassioned cheers, joined by the rebellious beat of the amassed runners, stamping their feet with exuberance. Ten years ago, Angelina was an apprentice runner, and, like now, she played her guitar to us all. I was so young. I never imagined that I would listen to her again, mesmerised by her minor chords and haunting riffs. For the first time, I feel proud of Pia, the reborn Pia, icon of #FutureProof, who enticed everyone here.

Angelina's echoing solo pierces the air, trembling in my ears until the sound fades across the clifftop towards the sea. Robin rises from her stool in the wings, appearing centre stage, to rapturous applause. She addresses us all. I listen attentively to her impassioned speech, desperate to play my part, cheering with the crowd. She rallies the troops, talking of the vital role played by the runners in connecting diverse communities, 'We succeeded with #Spoiler a decade ago. Now is the time for the runners to re-emerge, for those of you living in the earths to rise again, declaiming your unique ideology. We owe it to our fellow human beings …' The clapping drowns her final words, as the band strikes up while she walks carefully down among the runners, talking with friends, greeting strangers. They still love her. She is stirring their blood. This might just work …

Nathan takes to the stage to more waves of adoring applause. I don't want him to be so successful. Still struggling with the pain he has caused me, despite our upbeat rescue attempt, and my newfound pride in Pia.

Robin and Nathan take part in an apparently spontaneous dialogue over the microphones, throwing ideas into the crowd: *we are detoxifying our planet through sustainable action, collaboration and empowerment.* The runners reward their heroes with a resounding ovation, the whole clifftop echoing with potent and heart-felt rebellion. I'm not sure how Robin will be able to justify this as non-political under the new contract, but it is certainly uplifting for those of us already on board with the cause.

'So, what is #FutureProof?' Robin asks provocatively. Their phones are connected to the wifi microphones. Nathan organised it. As the runners shout out their contributions, their hopeful words echo across the clifftop, and appear on the big screens. There would have been a time when Robin would have lambasted all this tech, but Nathan is the blue-eyed boy now.

'You need to futureproof food production: the earths already provide locally sourced sustainable vegan meals for all their community members.'

'Futureproof waste: we need zero-waste communities everywhere, like the earths.'

'Futureproof is digital detox Nathan: virtuality is toxic …' My ears prick up. Nathan brushes off this comment with a shy smile, responding with, 'Pia is the ultimate in eco-heroes. We need her …'

'Futureproof must be sustainable: renewable energy, collaborative transport, an educated society aware of the risks … we must learn from the earths. It can be done.'

'Rewilding. It is simple.'

'Yes! Simple tech Nathan. Futureproof the tech …'

'Futureproof has to champion low-impact housing. It's essential …'

When a woman shouts out, *'Non-violent solutions to world problems,'* her words appearing instantly on the screens, I catch Miranda glancing anxiously at Robin.

But Robin responds with one of her eloquent speeches to end the session, 'Yes, friends, the earths are our inspiration and the runners will enable us to enjoy futureproofed years ahead. Without you all, this would not be possible. We can now prove that it works, that there are collaborative non-violent solutions to our human problems. We are committed to international cooperation, to investment in a non-violent future, where individuals are empowered in a truly democratic society, where despots are replaced with thinkers and committed people of action …' Miranda smirks. I wonder why. Robin continues, 'We will empower citizens. We will invest in future generations and we will work together *with* natural ecosystems to restore the balance of the planet. It will not be quick, or easy, but with de-escalation in material affluence, and with a determination to end exploitation, we can do this.'

Nathan adds, reflectively, 'We have not only taken our seat around the highest table, where world leaders plan the future on our behalf, but we will take control of that table to futureproof human life for generations to come.' He scans the crowd, his gaze falling intently upon me. Then the thing I dread most, happens, and he beckons me up on to the stage.

…………

They had prepared me for this. I grip the scrap of paper in the pocket of my best jeans, taking a deep breath as I am hustled through the cheering throng. 'Pia, Pia,' they chant in unison, as Angelina strums extracts of Pia theme tunes.

I scramble up, feeling clumsy, surveying the ocean of eager faces in the moonlight, knowing I am not Pia; but that they want Pia. Silence. Anticipation. I grip the scrap of paper, remembering what is scribbled on it.

'Friends, we must ensure Pia does not wield a double-edged sword. Her success must not cause tech to proliferate over basic human reason' Nathan has permitted me to say that, but my voice sounds young and feeble. I build my volume, 'Pia will help us to bring virtuality followers on board with our vision for Futureproof. I represent the next generation. I believe in Robin's vision for the planet, and we are all in this together.' My pre-prepared words tumble out awkwardly.

The runners look puzzled, but the mood is high, and once a few begin to clap, the others follow. I hurry off the stage to tumultuous confusion. Images of Pia are flashing on the screens. Robin and Nathan are ushered off the stage into the nearest dormitory. As Angelina strikes up on her guitar, I am hustled after Nathan. I catch Miranda's eye, and she gives a thumbs up, but she is looking behind me.

I turn and glimpse the Muddler. The Muddler from Tarquin. Miranda's accomplice. While I am trying to make sense of it all, they grip me in a vice-like hold. My hands are bound, a hood shoved over my head. I don't even fight back in my stunned surprise. I am bundled into some sort of vehicle and driven away at speed. Why? Who? Where are we going?

Desperate and immobile with fear, I feel around me. All I can use to orientate myself is smooth fabric of a seat in a vehicle. Slap! My hand is rapped firmly. I scream with surprise at the pain.

'Keep your hands to yourself you minx.' A coarse male voice.

Then a woman, 'If she causes you any trouble, just use the Forane.'

My brain is in overdrive. What is Forane? 'Don't you touch me,' I yell, and squirm, trying to shake my arms loose of the binding.

'I'm warning you.'

A musty smell … musty … swimming …

……….

I wake drowsily, and try to make sense of urgent voices.

'But we are ready. We need her *now*. She is the chosen one and she needs to be awake. Who gave her the stuff anyway?'

'Never mind that. She will be awake soon. Everything has gone according to plan.'

'Your plan you mean. Not my plan. Not Miranda's plan.'

'Fuck off.'

'Miranda said treat her well, but she is out of it. It's not good.'

'Let me see her.'

'What are you going to do?'

'Wake her up of course.'

'No damage. We need her intact.'

…………

The familiar face of The Muddler looms as she removes the hood, which is damp with my troubled breath. She peers down at me, assessing my condition. 'You okay Poppy?'

I refuse to respond, and remain silent.

'Don't play awkward with me. Here, have some water.' The Muddler retrieves a bottle of water from her bag, snapping open the plastic top. I never drink bottled water on principle, but my mouth is dry, my head swimming.

'Thank you.'

'Ah, you have a voice. Good.'

'Why am I here?'

'You'll find out in due course. Anything else you need?'

She is terse, minimal and unhelpful, but I desperately need an ally.

'You're Verna, aren't you?' I ask bravely.

'How the fuck do you know my name?'

I remember Miranda telling me, but I'm not going to admit that. 'I was at Tarquin. I heard someone … saw you.

I …'

'Ah. Tarquin. Okay. Are you in a fit state to appear?'

'Appear?'

'Yes, in the meeting. They want to see you before you do it.'

'Do what?'

'You'll see.'

I consider running, as my limbs are finally free, but I have no idea where I am, and someone is guarding the door. At the very instant that I glance hopefully at the door, a tall man with thinning grey hair pushes his way through, saying, 'Well I must see her first.'

Instinctively, I stand. I brush down my jeans, then tidy my hair with my hands.

'Poppy. My goodness.' He speaks with received pronunciation, moving with elegance. 'Poppy, I must apologise if this has been an unpleasant and unexpected experience for you. You are in my care now and I can assure you that you will be well looked after. You have an important role to play.'

Miranda's words: *an important role to play.*

'I don't think you know me, my dear. I am Reginald de Vere.

Robin's godfather. Miranda's boss, carrying a document wallet. The sender of the many Christmas presents to Caernef. The old guy that The Scurrilous and the Clinician were talking about. I remain passive. Still in shock. Clench my fists in my lap and wait.

'Is there anything you need before you meet the committee? They are ready for you. Then we will return you to your family and friends at Caernef.'

Robin likes this De Vere bloke. So does Miranda, I think. You can never be sure with her. His eyes look honest, which is odd, given the circumstances.

'Mr De Vere, before you take me into the committee, I need to know what is going on. Please explain.'

'Hasn't Miranda briefed you?'

'No … at least, I don't believe so.'

'It is #FutureProof. This is the highest managing authority. The future of the planet is hanging in the balance, and #FutureProof is the solution. The only solution. We are engaged in an ambitious global programme to overcome evil. It's complicated, Poppy. Miranda … your friend Miranda, is the chief negotiator. She is making incredible progress. It is confidential, which I am sure you understand. So, we find ourselves ready to invite you to play your part in #FutureProof.'

'And Robin's #FutureProof?'

A strange look passes across his face, and he frowns, while deciding what to say to me. 'Robin is a dreamer, well-intentioned and ideological. Not like her father at all. Robin believes in an ethical, sustainable future, and that is what we are honouring in #FutureProof.'

He is beginning to appear hassled and goes to rise from his seat. I want to establish myself on a level with him. Don't appreciate being talked down to. So I recite Miranda's quotation; *'Persons with any weight of character carry, like planets, their atmospheres along with them in their orbits.'*

'My goodness, Poppy, how do you know that?'

'Miranda wrote it on the parcel for Robin. The one containing the old copy of Return of the Native.'

'Ah, I see. Well, the time has come for you to play your part. It is a great honour that you have been chosen.'

'Who chose me?'

'So many questions, but if you must know, I did. I chose you. I chose Poppy Kiwan, the quiet, modest, child of Caernef. Come with me, Poppy, there is no need to be nervous.

He is frustratingly distinguished and alluring, so I abandon my reserve, letting him lead me by the hand through the doorway, into the underground chamber at Tarquin. At last, I know exactly where I am.

As we enter, around a dozen middle-aged and elderly men glide back into their chairs, a silence falling upon the company. Miranda said anti-establishment but it looks to me like the establishment itself, embodied in this sterile underground room without any links to the real world, to nature, creatures, the sky or the sea.

Their eyes turn on me. De Vere ushers me to the head of the table. 'This is Poppy, colleagues. She has come today to play her part.' They nod and look serious. My heart is banging, my brain whirring. What are they going to make me do?

In a silky-smooth voice, De Vere recites some words in another language. Latin, I think. They all bow their heads as if in prayer. God, this is weird. I notice the cameras. They are filming this.

'Poppy Kiwan, this is the moment for you to press the switch, enabling #FutureProof to proceed. Only you can activate the future. You represent the generations to come, and only your fingerprint will work. Today you are providing us with the blueprint. The future is dependent upon you.

As if in a dream, I am stupefied, and lean forwards. I imagine I am Pia, passing my gaze round the room, building the tension, staring at each serious face in turn. They do not hurry me. I raise the forefinger on my left hand over the digital pad in the centre of the table in front of De Vere. He nods at me, as if I am a small child, and I place my finger firmly on the digital switch, holding it there for a few seconds, before releasing it. An inaudible sigh travels the room. I step back, waiting for something to happen. I'm not sure what. But everything is the same. The faces. The table. The computer screens and the cameras. With me, small, and confused. When I turn towards the door, I catch a view of the Muddler. She bustles in, gripping my arm. *Carpe Diem. Prope est finis mundi …*

…………

The bare bulbs in the dormitory pierce the back of my eyes with a strange pain, and I sit up, holding my head.

'Blimey Pops, you look rough. What were you drinking

last night? Mum and Dad were worried, but I covered for you.'

Cai, loyal and dependable. Here when I need him. But I'm confused.

'I didn't drink anything.' The words seem reluctant to come out of my mouth.

'How about I grab you a coffee. You look like you could do with one.'

'Thanks Cai. I feel - sort of odd - but okay. I think.' I don't want him to leave me, and shut my eyes for the comfort of the darkness. Trying to recall what happened, but it is all a blur. Maybe my drink was spiked. But I don't remember drinking anything at all. Just water. Bottled water?

I peep out from between my eyelids. The dormitory is empty. Runner's belongings, rucksacks, abandoned sleepwear, guitars and blankets. The debris of a good night, no doubt. I remember Robin's speech, as well as Nathan … of course; it was the great event last night. I must have just fallen asleep in the dormitory with the others.

'Here you go Poppy. Get this down you.'

'You sound like Dad.'

'Ha. There's breakfast out in the parade ground. Vegan bacon rolls. I've had two.'

I can smell the waft of frying food. Nothing beats breakfast outside. I slurp the coffee and follow Cai towards the clifftop, where the air is still chill from an overnight dip in temperature.

The parade ground is filled with makeshift stalls bartering for breakfast. Every single firepit is being used, with hundreds of runners gathering on the logs, round the fires and simply sitting on the grass staring out towards the estuary. The mood is upbeat with a buzz of conversation. Buried in this hopeful crowd is Robin, her hands gripping a cup of tea, her face optimistic. Today there will be workshops, old-style, and then by lunchtime, everyone will depart.

As soon as I am spotted, chants of 'Pia, Pia,' start up. Cai takes my hand, ushering me through the smoke towards the arcade, swapping a virtuality card of Pia, signed by Nathan, for two breakfast rolls. Leaving the crowds behind us, we settle on the clifftop and eat. Cai's third of the morning.

'So, Poppy, where *were* you last night?'

I consider his question carefully, but cannot recall anything other than drinking from a bottle of water. 'Cai, I really don't know. Honestly. It's odd …' I can tell he doesn't believe me. I brush crumbs off my jeans, and spot burdock seeds clinging to the bottoms of the legs.

'Tarquin?'

'What?'

'Tarquin. That's where I kept collecting burdock seeds on my clothes. They just stick on when you go past. There's no burdock here at Caernef. At least, I don't think so. Have you ever seen any, Cai?'

'What's burdock?'

'Never mind. What's the plan for this morning?'

…………

Caernef was perfect today. A fresh salty breeze but no rain. The runners took over the parade ground, and representatives from the earths toured the allotments, surveying the alternative energy installations with keen interest. The dormitories filled with impromptu music. Wherever we went, Cai and I were offered cups of tea accompanied by spiced biscuits. The pledge for action grew and grew through the morning, as Robin's collaboration to #FutureProof the planet became a reality.

But I was consumed with a nagging suspicion that some trickery had been enacted during the night. I don't know what or how, but I'm uncomfortable. The event has closed, with rousing speeches, and mercifully I could observe rather than be hoist on to the stage. If Robin can pull this off, and she has, of course, done it before, if she can, then I will have so much more confidence in a grassroots-inspired future whereby humans abandon conflict and co-exist with nature.

The event has kick-started Robin's new campaign. She has Nathan back on board, with his contacts, committees and funds, so #FutureProof is buoyant, but while Miranda is lurking in the wings, I am increasingly uneasy. I'm still not sure what happened to me, on the night of the runner's festival. Cai thinks my drink was spiked, but why would I drink bottled water. I never do. And there were the burrs on my trousers. Tarquin. I'm sure.

10: FUTURE GALACTIC

Rio solves the mystery for me. I'm booked in for another stint of character writing in Cyber City. She sends me a briefing note a few days ahead of my arrival, and it blows my mind. *Pia III: Final Scene: operator solution: discover Pia fingerprint on switch enables blast off. Survival mission. Leads into galactic post-Pia hero to succeed series. Pia handover to successor.*

This is vitally important for me. Firstly, Nathan has honoured my demand for Pia III to be her final adventure, and secondly, it has prompted my memory. If I concentrate hard, I can at last remember some of what happened to me on that bizarre night when I think I was drugged. I looked around the Tarquin boardroom, gazing, stunned, at the faces of old men, wondering about the ruling classes and *the establishment,* and they told me to place my finger on the switch. But nothing happened. That man De Vere was in charge. What is he up to? Is Miranda involved or not? Am I somehow, through virtuality, writing myself out of reality?

....

Rio has been delayed – something about Nathan, so I have planted myself in front of the developer screens. I won't start without her, but I will try to log in. I intend to get a feel for the next section. Keen to view the denouement of Pia III, I go for it. She has left me a scrawled password on a scrap of paper, tucked under the router. Unfolding it, I read, 49909-008. I log in and pop the note into the pocket of my jeans.

The computer is already open on a work-in-progress. The timeline is set to the future, too far ahead for my work, in something called *Future Galactic*. I'm not at all interested in a galactic future, but have a peek. The scenes are only sketched with the sepia tones of Nathan's characteristic draft mode, and I just want to exit, but something draws me in …

…two simultaneous screens. On the left is utter devastation. Like there has been a war, or a massive bomb. Gazing intently, I perceive a familiar view, which has become ravaged by a fiery wind. Dawning realisation that this scene means too much to be ignored. The wooden planks cladding the Caernef dormitories are heaped in piles of glowing ash, and there are piles of … bodies … on the parade ground. It's like my clifftop home has become Pompeii. The programmers have even added the reek of burning vegetation, the sound of shrieking creatures and the eerie beat of a solitary drum, counting time, but slowing.

… meanwhile on the right-hand side of the screen a cyber shuttle is undocking. Automatic zoom and there are diplomats belted into their space seats, with jolly flags adding a burst of colour along the aisles. I press the zoom and squint at the sketched faces of The Clinician, the Scurrilous and … an upright gentleman sat directly under the Union Jack. A vaguely familiar face. Carrying a document case. De Vere.

I press my finger on the escape button at the very same millisecond that Rio breezes into the room. Something odd about her today. A tinge of embarrassment, or guilt.

'Hi Poppy, how lovely to see you again. Now, we need to set up the finale of Pia III. I'm so looking forward to it.'

Rio is full of ideas. She has been in endless meetings with Nathan, and she knows exactly how he wants to wind up Pia, his biggest success, ready to transition to the next enterprise, which he hopes will be even more popular. The soundtrack is already complete, and we can stretch it, or compact sections, using the software. I love this. It's like painting a picture with the music.

Today, we focus on the minute details, getting the environment perfect, and then, after a lunch break, we start to shape the last few days of Pia herself.

'Nathan wants some sort of martyrdom scene.'

'Martyrdom?'

'Yes, like she is sacrificing her life for the future of the human race. That sort of thing.'

For Rio, this is just a cybergame. A very good, very successful cybergame. For Nathan, this is an even bigger sacrifice. He is killing his imaginary soulmate. Nathan knows he should never have used me. He needs an out from Pia, despite his passion for his virtual friend. Thank goodness I spoke up. This so needs doing.

'You okay about this, Poppy? I mean, it's like you are planning your own death … in a way.'

'Rio, it's what I want. You know that.' I reassure her. So, we design the scenes, we develop the character, setting up the final scenario. I imagine Cai operating, and I want him to be impressed.

'Pia is going to discover the key to the future of the human race. The sequence will be imprinted on her fingertip, and she will end up on the top of Mount Ceòlm.'

'But she will not know, until the very last minute; it isn't only her finger that is needed, so she will sacrifice her whole body …'

'… which is of course virtual, Poppy my friend …'

'Yes, but that doesn't matter. She has to decide in a split second, whether to self-destruct, and to give the scientists the fingerprint, or whether to quit, to take the imprint away, and to hide for the rest of her life, hoping they won't find her.'

'At first, Nathan wanted the second option.' Rio tells me.

'I'm sure he did. He doesn't want Pia to end, ever. But

Rio, is Nathan okay with our ending, or will he simply over-write it when we pass it back to him?'

'I trust Nathan, Poppy. He will run with our ending. He has changed …his mind is on the next game already. Pia is old news.'

Why do I feel disappointed? I am ashamed as I discover I secretly enjoyed Nathan's infatuation with an image of me. Suddenly doubting my determination to end Pia, I hesitate … not because I want more royalties. They are irrelevant. In fact, I don't want the money at all. But I realise that, through Pia, I became the force for change that I had always hoped to be. Pia is the ultimate campaigner, effective, powerful, loved. Pia is graceful and fast, unlike me. Pia is the successor to the ethical Robin and the cutthroat Miranda. Can I let her go? Do I want to return to being alone and unimportant?

We work on the final scene for hours. We create a knowing look on Pia's face as she plants her finger on the fingerprint reader, and as the screen fills with the overblown explosions of fireworks that all gameplayers seek. It's done. She's gone. Digital funeral pyre. Beautiful and exhausted silence.

'Now Poppy, is there anything you want to go back over. Any scenes to rework?'

'You know, Rio, I don't think I can. Finally, she is gone. I need to make the break. To tell the truth, I'm emotionally exhausted by it all. Relieved too.'

Rio hits *save* and two seconds later, Nathan appears in the doorway, asking if it is done.

'Yes.' We both say simultaneously. Rio, with triumph, and me with an uneasy satisfaction.

'You won't change it will you Nathan?' I ask.

'No. I promise. It will stand just as you and Rio have created it, with a bit of tidying up if needed. Anyway, Poppy, this is for you.'

Nathan hands me a bijou jewellery box, tied with a blue ribbon. This is Rio's work, I know it. I undo the ribbon, peeping inside. A silver frond of whin, on a fine chain. It is utterly beautiful. 'Thank you, Nathan,' I say, with feeling.

'I should be thanking you. Your work with Rio on Pia is fantastic. Thank you, Poppy.'

I need fresh air. Need to get completely clear of virtuality. I hug Rio, nod shyly at Nathan, collect my bag, clutch the jewellery box, and walk through the door. Glancing back into the pristine room where so much has been created, I glimpse Rio and Nathan's heads close together, pouring over the screen.

I go. But Cyber City does not offer the immediate respite I need. I don't ever want to set foot in this place again. I long for Caernef. Want to be home, far away from the massive hoardings advertising *Pia III, the ultimate*, far away from the detritus of throwaway living littering the streets, far away from the people who are plugged in 24/7 but who still find time to glare at me, jeering *paedo Pia* as I pass. They don't know who I am. Just think I look like her by accident I suppose. There is no place for me here. I only feel a connection with the weeds struggling through the paving. Misshapen celandine and the occasional violet providing scattered yellow and purple in an otherwise grey desert.

....

On my return, the task complete, Rio satisfied, and Pia finished forever, I decide I must confide in Cai. However, when I bound up the stairs, jumping on to my bed, he is completely immersed in one of Pia III's earlier challenges, and my bed is piled high with his boxes and crumby paper bags from the Caernef bakery.

'Don't tell me the ending Pops. Whatever you do, don't tell me. I'm nearly there. Only a few more days and I'll be on the final scene. Nathan says I'm the furthest ahead of anybody. Ciel's way behind me; all the forums are still talking about Pia II. And he told me he has a *new* girlfriend …'

I smile, despairingly, wonder about the *girlfriend*, hand

Cai the coffee from Mum, then decide to slink down the stairs, worries heaped upon my shoulders.

Even though it is late, I head for the arcade, holding Nathan's jewellery box tightly, as I jog down the path. I stash the exquisite whin necklace, in its box, alongside Miranda's phone, under the redundant platform. They fit neatly in my favourite box, which I have filled with my prize finds; feathers, dried leaves, seed pods.

Anyway, now Pia is behind me, I have another important task to perform. I have slogged away on the four science modules throughout the year, mostly studying alone, online and begrudgingly. This term we have end of year exams, and I have struck a deal with Dad that if I pass with flying colours, I can discuss different options for next year, so I need to devote all the time I can to revision. I'm determined. Miranda's guidance echoes through my head: *'Take control. Don't let* them *push you around.'*

....

Yesterday Cai helped me to clear up the arcade. We worked all day, taking sack loads of Nathan's old stuff to the quarry, where we buried it. I swept so vigorously that dust billowed out of the doorway in clouds. We scraped the muck off the floor so it has become lovely clean concrete, laid by a farmer fifty years ago. We have also removed handfuls of spider's webs.

All my collections are still safe inside, but tidy and organised rather than the chaotic jumble of my childhood. Having totally dismantled Nathan's once-glowing platform, we set up his old workbench as a desk, so I can do all my revision down here. Robin found an ancient primus stove that works remarkably well, which runs off white gas. With a screen for the wind, and a camping kettle, I can brew up outside whenever I want. I feel like a nomadic student in a Caernef bubble, reading books old-style, while all my friends plug in to the *progressive* digital society.

....

Pia III is an even greater success than Pia II. The scenes Rio and I wrote are going down a storm. Cai finished playing Pia III only a week after it launched, with 24-hour sessions, much derided by Mum. So, in his eyes, Pia is gone. He is already looking forward to Future Galactic, like so many other dedicated virtuality fanatics.

I have completely switched off from all of that, and the remainder of the academic year is hurrying by. Revising science until my brain is so crammed with facts, it feels as if it will burst. I'm not focusing on anything other than my studies, and have almost forgotten about Pia. I go into school as infrequently as possible, just once a fortnight for a quick face-to-face catch up with teachers. My diligence has put me in Mum's good books; she is even baking me cakes to keep my energy up.

But I will have to go into school for the actual exams, and there's only a few more days before the first paper. It's environmental biology. I'm ready.

....

Trouping into the examination hall is like something out of history. After all the tech learning, testing us in this way seems an anachronism. Body scans, separate desks, no access to any of the tech props my friends have used throughout their lives. I pass the cameras and am sent, through facial recognition, to a desk in the centre of the room, where I sit, trying to calm my nerves. I don't know the teacher in charge. He marches up and down, glaring at anyone who makes a noise.

The silence of expectation. I'm hoping for questions on dynamic ecosystems, and community ecology as I have loads of examples, but I'm not as good at genetic modification. Why don't they begin? The hands on the clock creep to nine o'clock. A bell sounds, so we automatically, and obediently, turn over the papers on our desks. I scan the questions, smile to myself, grip the regulation pen and dive in.

How on earth can two hours pass in the blink of an

eye. Only two minutes left, I place the pen on the desk, and check my answers. Don't need to change anything. The bell sounds, and the glaring teacher dismisses us. The automated assistant begins to collect the papers as we file out of the hall in silence.

The moment we burst into the corridor, there is a cacophonous clamouring of voices. They are holding their heads, complaining about the questions, rubbing their tired hands, not used to so much writing. As that's my only exam today, I'm keen to get home to Caernef, and revise for tomorrow's biodiversity paper.

'Hi, Poppy, isn't it? I'm Rick.

I know him with a passing interest. He usually sits at the back of the room, when I do come into class, which hasn't been often lately. He probably wants to talk to me about Pia. They usually do.

'Hi,' I continue walking towards the door, Miranda-style.

'Come for a coffee, Poppy. I want to ask you something.'

Oh God. Maybe he fancies me. Better wriggle out of this. 'I'm due back at Caernef …' I begin.

'Ah. It won't take long. Miss Davies suggested I talked to you because I am thinking of switching to English next year. Not many people do it, but she said you might too. Do you want to?'

His deep brown eyes seem trustworthy, and he speaks with a shyness that I find reassuring. 'Yes, to both: the coffee, and I want to switch.'

We laugh, as I follow him, striding towards the coffee bar. 'I have it black. Plant milk?' He buys for me.

'But I don't think I have the courage to. I mean, Mum and Dad want me to carry on, specialising in ecology; especially *Futureproof the Planet* modules. But my heart isn't in it. I just find it all depressing. What about you Rick?'

We perch on a low wall, watching the stragglers from the exam disappear round the corner, phones in hands. I realise that, like me, he isn't holding a phone, furthermore, I am witnessing another person struggling for words more than I do. I wait patiently for his reply, blowing my coffee to cool it down.

'I've been plucking up the courage to speak to you for weeks. Yan and Bea said just message you, but I don't think you do that stuff.'

'No, and I haven't been in much. Been revising at home.'

'I read about Caernef. It must be awesome to actually live there.'

'It's all I've known. It's sort of … normal … for me.' I explain.

He rummages in his rucksack, pulling out a notebook. 'Look.'

His sketches are good. Mostly futuristic space and gaming, but accomplished, and I compliment him.

He flips through the pages, and settles on one that he removes carefully, and hands to me. 'For you.'

'Thanks Rick!' I study his pencil sketch of a magnificent sea eagle. 'Have you ever seen one?'

'Yes. I went to the centre for endangered species in Birmingham. It was amazing.'

'But not in the wild.'

He laughs, 'No. Of course not.'

'Would you like to see one in the wild?' I ask, wondering whether I will regret this invitation.

'Would I? Like on those video tours they advertise?'

'No. I know where one hunts. I could take you there some day.'

He doesn't need to answer as his eyes widen, his mouth opens, and for a few moments, he is lost for words. 'Yes please.'

'How about when exams finish?'

'You promise?'

''I do.'

…………

In my mind, promises mustn't ever be broken, so I am walking to the station just down the hill from home. Usually, a walk to the station means a trip to find Miranda, but not today. Very few trains call here. However, you can still request a stop, which is what I have told Rick to do. His final physics exam was this morning. I did ecology instead, so I finished yesterday. My *friends* are over-the-top excited. Much drinking and virtualityfests. I left college quickly after my exam, to escape any more invitations.

The station is unchanged since I was young. It stays in a bubble of old-world, a bit like Caernef, and the earths of course. Weeds push their way through the decaying concrete. A clump of scarlet pimpernel tells me the afternoon will be sunny, while banks of willowherb send fluffy seeds into the air, spinning and twirling in the breeze. Lichen has grown over the graffiti, and paint peels off an old sign saying *Alight here for Caernef Camp* so the wording is barely visible. *We want to be in a forgotten backwater*, Robin says. Even so, a neat new Caernef Enterprises sign has been attached to the rain shelter, showing guests the way to walk, giving Dad's work number if they want to be collected: I can still discern the shape of the previous, massive, Executive Property notice, a scalloped ghost on the shiplap.

As I cross the footbridge, kicking last year's fir cones, I hear a train slowing, and suddenly, there he is, in person, a geeky student blinking in the sunlight. Nervous and excited all at once, I wave, and we smile. The train disappears in the direction of England, but it has sixty miles to go, through fields, past forests and castles.

'Have you ever been on this line before?' I ask Rick, to break the embarrassment.

'No, but I'd like to …'

'Come on!' I lead the way at my usual brisk pace, past the Douglas Fir and up the hill. Rick is panting. He is obviously not used to walking, like the other virtuality addicts, so just where you can glimpse the estuary over the fields, I pause to let him catch his breath. We stand in silence, while the sun disappears behind a skein of cirrostratus, and re-emerges. He seems impressed.

'How was your physics?'

'Gruesome.'

'Oh. Sorry.'

'It's not too late to change subjects for next year. I want to talk about it.'

'Go on then …' I encourage, but he waits until the gradient flattens out.

'I don't want to be the only one Poppy. I mean, if we both switched, it would seem more … normal.'

'Haha!' I laugh, 'I don't think people see me as *normal*.'

'Maybe not, but they respect you. You have principles and you stick to them. My dad s likes that.'

God, he has told his dad about me. I wince. We walk in silence through the top gates to Caernef, and I show him how to pass through the security scanners, hidden in a neat wooden hut above the parade ground. We wait in the sunshine.

'What's the hold up?' He asks politely.

'Don't worry, it scans databases. Takes a while. Soon you will be issued with a day pass … oh, here it is.' The machine whirrs and Rick's photo ID emerges. He picks up a lanyard, clipping it on, so we are free to roam. I take him on the standard tour, visiting the ecofarm, the education centre, the allotments, skirting the clifftop, indicating home across the tussocks - avoiding my parents - and leading him towards the arcade …

'Hi Pops, who's this then?'

11: SEA EAGLE

After a brief conversation with Cai, who, sensing my nervousness, isn't mischievous enough to detain us, I lead Rick past the arcade, informing him with forced bravado how I adopted it, years ago, as my own private space.

Rick studies the dilapidated wooden slats, which perform the function of walls, the decaying window frames and the odd corrugated iron lean-to. He raises his eyebrows, commenting, 'I know it inside, of course. It's just like in virtuality. In real life, it's straight out of a history book. Didn't know places like this still existed, except in games, of course.'

He attempts to change our course, seemingly keen to look inside, but I don't trust him enough yet, and use my willpower to continue walking towards the cliff edge, hoping desperately he will follow me.

Rick peers across a mass of cobwebs, through the front window of the arcade. It's changed, of course, since Nathan stole it to generate more millions. Had a massive clean-up. Seeing me striding ahead, Rick runs to catch up.

'Poppy, I need to know …'

I freeze, motioning to him to join me in silence. His sentence hangs in the air, as he creeps across the carpet of thrift with over-exaggerated steps. This all a game to him. He hasn't noticed that, in the distance, the white-tailed eagle is diving on to the boiling surface of the sea, soaring upwards, then swooping down at speed, silhouetted against the sun.

Rick follows my gaze. 'Fucking hell.'

'I said we would see him. He comes each day at this time.'

'I didn't believe you. Didn't hope …'

'If we sit quietly, he might come closer.'

Slowly, we sink down on to a smooth rock, fringed in lichen; a comfortable seat, which I have used many times. For at least five minutes, we remain silent, watching the majestic bird performing his show. The sun disappears behind the clouds, and we stop squinting, as the sea eagle works his patch, coming closer and closer.

I never cease to be amazed by the size of this bird. I think it is a male because it's smaller than the other eagle I sometimes see. Occasionally I see a pair. They say the wings are like a barn door, spanning around eight feet. He soars over the estuary, piercing eyes on the look-out for fish. We are mesmerised as he glides so close to us, his yellow hooked beak, his strange talons tucked up, ready to flip out, to snare his prey. When this top predator is around, the skies tend to be quiet. The estuary birds take cover, waiting for their turn.

Rick is enthralled, following his every move, totally unaware of anything other than our enormous bird. The eagle has spotted something, and wheels back, soaring lower and lower, when with a flick, he skims the surface of the water, climbing on an air current, with a hefty fish in his claws. Perhaps it is a young bass or pollack. Might even be a cod.

Suddenly an alarm sounds from the quarry, across the estuary. The shrill shriek sends the eagle high into the air, and we watch him sail powerfully out of view, carrying his booty back towards the furthest peninsula on the edge of Wales.

Silence.

For an awkward moment, I fear Rick is going to kiss me, but he grips my shoulders exultantly, thanking me. He is totally won over by the beautiful bird.

'If only I had my phone,' he observes.

That is why Rick is not for me. He is weak; dependent. I need him only as a co-conspirator; so we can switch to studying the subjects we both crave.

'You don't need your phone, Rick,' I retort.

Amazed and abashed, he shrugs, gazing into the far distance, perhaps hoping the eagle will return. But we have had our treat for today. He tends not to return the same day, so once he disappears, I generally know when the show is over.

....

As we walk briskly away from Caernef, towards the station, the magic has come and gone, and Rick is brusque. I think he se senses I disapprove of him. Can't make me out.

In an attempt to break the awkwardness, I return to the subject of college, pledging my support for him in his quest to switch his options, emphasizing how it is art that will change the world for the better, in a way that science has failed; failed to capture the collective human imagination sufficiently to halt the tide of abuse of our once-beautiful planet.

'The trouble is, Poppy,' he mutters, 'The trouble is, you are so caught up in the big picture, that you are … well, to be honest … it's all a fantasy.

Does he mean our fledgeling relationship? Does he mean my life? I hold my initial reaction, breathe, asking, with a masquerade of calmness, 'How do you mean?'

'All this about changing the world. How many of us have said it, knowing that in reality, we are just small people, without influence, without power, and without resource to make any difference at all. It's crap; we cannot change the world. That's why we need art; music, fantasy games, to escape the harsh reality of the hopelessness of our existence. That's what's real, I'm afraid Poppy. Your Robin is just a middle-aged hippy. She has a comfortable life, after all. Doesn't know what it's really like not to have much.'

I wonder who has said that about Robin to him. 'And Miranda?' I ask.

'Who's Miranda?'

'She's the opposite of Robin. Miranda is … well, changing the world order through #FutureProof,' I volunteer.

'Did she study art or science?' he retorts, with a sneer. 'Come on, Poppy, we are just insignificant. You, me, Robin, and this *Miranda*.'

Rick looks at his feet, then his phone. I look at my watch. The train is due any minute. We hurry down the steps to the platform just in time, waving frantically to request a stop.

Perhaps he is right.

'Thanks for today, Poppy. It has been real special. I will always remember that fantastic bird …'

He bends towards me, and kisses me on the cheek. Then, hurriedly disappears into the train.

…………

After rubbing my cheek clean with my sleeve, and running back home, being Miranda of course, I hurtle through the Caernef gates. As I dash round the corner by the kitchens, my mind on other things, I literally bump into Robin. Unusually, she is out and about, strolling across the parade ground.

'Poppy, slow down dear!'

'Sorry, I was miles away.'

'Who was the delightful young gentleman I saw, accompanying you out on the clifftop this afternoon?'

Robin and her binoculars. 'Just Rick; someone from college. He's into sea eagles.'

'Ah yes?' She thinks he is my boyfriend.

'Actually, Rick and I are hoping to switch our options next year. I've had it with science Robin. What do you think?'

She looks for somewhere to sit, and we straddle the

tree trunks by the dead embers in the fire pit. Stirring the cold ashes with her stick, Robin considers her words. 'I think you stand in the centre of a crossroads. Two ways lie behind you; your studies and your passions. Two roads lie ahead. Either you can remain loyal to Caernef, your home, your family, and our ideals, or you can forge a new future for yourself. You're at that age now Poppy, when you can choose …'

'Robin, do you believe that, as tiny individuals, we have the power to shape the future of the planet? Or is it all simply too big, and we are too small?'

'What's brought that on now? Of course we can shape the future, especially you. You have health and time on your side. Unlike me.'

'Last year you were far more pessimistic.'

'Now we have the runners back. Caernef is our own again. Thanks to Nathan, to Pia, and, of course, to you. The future is in our hands.'

'#FutureProof?'

'My #FutureProof. Yes.'

'And Miranda's? Miranda's #FutureProof?'

'As usual, Miranda is punching above her weight. She means well, but there is a limit to what she will achieve, cavorting with world leaders and plotting behind their backs. I know her game, and it's a thousand to one it will work. If it does, then ….'

'You used to tell us we must aim high, stretch up for the sky. You used to say to the runners that anything would be possible.'

'Oh Poppy, perhaps I am becoming the cynic these days. Or perhaps we are too far down a slippery slope … but your Miranda thinks she can change the world order. She's ambitious and foolhardy.'

I touch the scrap of paper in my pocket, and decide to ask her about the password. Robin knows about these things. Although I have learnt it by heart, I pull the note out of my jeans' pocket and show it to her. 'Robin, does this mean anything to you?'

'Indeed, it does! Well! Why do you want to know?'

'Just curious I suppose. I found it at Cyber City.'

'That den of iniquity. Well, Nathan always did believe he really stopped the glitch. Would you like to see it? It is all recorded in *Anna Karenina.*'

I walk slowly alongside Robin, stopping when she rests, not badgering her, until we eventually reach the folly. She wanders in, sits on the bottom of the stairs to catch her breath, then hauls herself up the stairs. She sits on the bed gesturing for me to stand on her chair, to reach the loft hatch. The ceiling is low. I push the hatch up and, as directed by Robin, feel around the edge until my hand touches a book. I assume it is *Return of the Native*, but when I pull it down, replacing the hatch, I can see it is, indeed, Robin's old copy of *Anna Karenina.* I hand I to her.

She cradles the book in her arms, sighs, and flicks through the pages, pausing upon a page near the end. She peers, closing one eye, squinting at the tiny words, then motioning for me to draw nearer. In the dim light, I can see miniscule scribbled notes, in pencil, and in different hands, weaving in and out of the original text.

'Here, Poppy, look!'

I squint at the scrawl, and read aloud, 'Nathan's guess to #stoptheglitch 008 49909; Poppy Boo (backwards), but no, it wasn't this after all, though I let him believe he had cracked it. The successful word was simply *peekaboo.* The rebel Tod Humboldt and Poppy played peekaboo at Caernef. So simple.'

'So simple,' Robin muses.

'I think I can remember playing peekaboo with strange men on the balcony outside the dormitory. They asked me my name. I had my yellow wellies on.'

'That's right. You were very young. Reginald staged secret diplomatic talks here at Caernef. They arrived by helicopter. You were meant to be kept out of sight, but your Mum took you out for some fresh air. They called you over.'

'I have many strange early memories. I once saw Miranda dressed as the enemy …'

'You did. Not long after that game of peekaboo.'

'Why, Robin?'

'Miranda wanted to push Year Zero even then. She was infatuated with Karl Campbell. She took us all prisoner for a while, here at Caernef, but she came to her senses, eventually.'

She is still determined to get us back to Year Zero.'

'Indeed.'

…………

Waiting for me on the doorstep at home are Mum and Dad, looking serious. No doubt they saw me with Rick, so I am going to get a lecture on the *Facts of Life*. Caernef is a goldfish bowl. Robin is right. I need more space. Freedom. Agency.

'Poppy, we need to talk,' Dad's gentle voice entices me. The three of us move indoors and sit by the fireplace, which still reeks from last year's fires. He winks at Mum. She smiles at him. Dad turns to me, 'Mum and I have been talking about your studies. We understand your point of view, and although it wouldn't be what we would do, given that you absolutely smashed your first year …'

I don't believe this is happening.

'… given that you absolutely smashed your first year, we will support you if you decide to change to studying arts.'

'In exchange, you want me to …?'

'No, no conditions. You are your own woman now Poppy.'

A comfortable pause hangs in the air while Mum and Dad crave my smiles again. They are making this massive gesture. Why?

'Why?'

'Because we love you, I guess,' Mum chimes in.

I hug Dad. I hug Mum. I rush upstairs to tell Cai, and I

text Rick. A huge heavy burden has been lifted from my shoulders. It has weighed me down for so long, I can hardly believe it is completely gone.

Launching into action immediately, I text my tutor, complete the application forms, obtain digital signatures. I can *do* digital if I need to. I just choose not to most of the time. I download the reading lists, opt for real books, withdraw every penny I earned from my stint at Tarquin, order the titles, and start researching course details online. I am totally obsessed.

I'm waiting at the top of the drive where deliveries are left in the Caernef post room, which is really a wooden hut smelling of paper and cedar, with old-style pigeon-holes for the post, and a huge wicker basket for parcels. Even here, drone deliveries are the norm now, rather than runners, although we are one of the final drops, so it is nearly lunchtime when I discern the distant whirring of today's Unmanned Aerial Delivery Vehicle. My books arrive.

I spend the final two weeks of the summer break reading. I drag myself out of bed really early each day, stumble to the arcade, brew up, and the days race by as I sit in the sun with my books. I am in arcadia. Life is perfect. I forget to eat, return home late, and everyone at home is pleased with me.

The first module links beautifully with last year's eco-sciences. It crosses disciplines, covering music, dance, drama, poetry, fine art, modern art and literature. You can choose five areas, but I am going to study all seven. It is right up my street; 'A comparison between art in the Romantic era and art of the mid twenty-first century eco/techno crisis.' Art means *all creative activity*; not just drawings and paintings. It is mega. I might even use Pia's character in virtuality to exemplify escapism from our mid-century crisis.

Rick and I will re-join the first year. Term starts in a week's time. Never have I so looked forward to school …

to college. Studying *my* chosen subjects in my own way.

....

'So Rick and I sat at the back, because we are the oldest, and I kicked off the discussion.' I had practised to myself for days, remembering all the points I wanted to make. 'I started by drawing on all the old stuff; you know; the Victorians who were suspicious of industrialisation way back. Ruskin, William Morris and Dickens' Coketown.'

Mum hands round the plates of supper, smiling at my enthusiasm through the steam. Cai wants to know about Ruskin; he has never heard of him. Dad has, 'Ruskin said that your reward for your work is not the money, but what you become by it. I sometimes think about him when I am working in the allotments.' Didn't know that Dad knew about this stuff too.

'Then Rick drew the parallels with protest art today. He knows all about it, even if he doesn't believe it will make any difference in the long run.'

Mum joins in, 'When you were a baby, Poppy, before Cai was born, we used to take you to the art gallery in Birmingham. Even then, you loved gazing at the paintings. Do you remember, Thomas, we used to walk round the Pre-Raphaelites to keep warm?'

'I do indeed.'

'I wish I could remember.'

'You were a baby, Poppy.'

'Before Caernef.'

I dig into my dinner. Even the interminable vegetables taste good, now I am happier at college. But I have so much homework, and the evenings are closing in, so the arcade is cold and dark. It's my turn to do the dishes.

As I race through the washing up at breakneck speed, an unusual shadow passes outside the window. I peer out, wondering whether it was a bird, or a bat, but it is getting dim already, so I decide to head to the arcade for the final hour or so of daylight.

With a spring in my step, I gaze at the pretty but

disturbing haze of red on the horizon, then trot down the path.

But someone has reached the arcade before me. I can hear the rattle of Nathan's old generator, and a light is flickering inside. A shadow. An outline, hazy through the cobwebs across the cracked glass. Is it? It can't be …

I burst through the door and come face to face with Miranda. Dressed in black, she forms a sinister figure, creeping around secretly. Like in the past.

'Poppy! At last!'

'Miranda?'

'We need you, Poppy; earlier than we thought, but right now, we need you.'

'You couldn't come in the usual way, say hello at home, and speak with me there? You couldn't message me even?'

'Not this time.'

'I'm busy Miranda. For the first time in years, I'm really busy, doing what I want to do, at last.'

'What is more important, Poppy, your small life, or saving the world; saving nature? Saving habitats, creatures. You always said that was most important to you.'

'But.'

'God, it's a boyfriend?'

'No. No. Rick's just a friend. I've just started back at college. The course is mega brilliant, and tonight I have *piles* of homework …'

'I'm afraid the homework will have to wait. We need to move, and quickly. You must come up with a reason, explain to your parents. Meet me at the station. My car's there. I don't want to get tangled up with Robin or the others just now. Poppy? Poppy, are you listening?'

'And if I say I won't?'

'Not an option.'

'What's in it for me then?'

'To play your part in #FutureProof. A vital part. Poppy, we need you more than you can know. I'm not giving you the choice here.'

The arcade is filled with the yellow light of an old-style electric bulb. Miranda's sinister figure casts long dark shadows on the walls. All my things, my collections, my books, lure me back, but at the same time, Miranda exudes a magnetic power. Didn't I always tell myself I wanted to escape Caernef for the wider world? Well, maybe this is my chance.'

Miranda is tense, 'Am I going to have to take you by force? I don't want to … you're too grown-up for that sort of behaviour now.'

Robin said there were two paths ahead. I want to forge my own future. I'm not timid Poppy Kiwan any more. I'm … I'm … certainly not Pia … I'm not Miranda either.

Miranda glimpses something in my collection boxes, and pounces. It's Arcadian B. She places it on her hand, waiting for me, just like we used to, when I was a child.

'Come on Poppy. It is your destiny. Take Arcadian B in your pocket, and you can do anything. Anything at all.'

'No.'

I run out of the open door of the arcade. With a slight head-start I am in with a chance. She powers behind, but this time I know I can beat her. The turning of the tide. Hold my breath as I run the fastest ever in my life. Miranda's strong arms flail desperately in my direction, but I manage to elude her. Turn the corner towards the lights of home.

'Shit Poppy!' sounds behind me, followed by a muffled call, 'I'll be at the station in an hour.'

I'm home.

…………

Mum calls from the sitting room, 'Thought you'd got a lot of homework.'

'I forgot a book,' I lie. Hate lying. Head upstairs.

'Cai, I need your help. It's urgent.' Not even time to think about this, but make sure I sound calm. Relaxed even.

Cai swings round from his screen and smiles

innocently, 'No worries. What can I do?'

'You know *Future Galactic*? Well, how far have you got?'

'Halfway through Part Three. They are all queuing up for the flight to the future. It's really ace Pops. You want to join in?'

'Haha, no thanks Cai. I just wanted to know what was on the horizon, for a friend.'

Cai frowns. He knows that Rick plays Future Galactic, and Cai is competitive.

'It's okay. Not Rick. Actually, I need to know for me.' *Keep it simple Poppy. Keep to the truth when you can.* I reach up to the shelf and grab Chap. 'Cai, I need to tell you something confidential; can we swear secrecy on Chap's life?' I ask, feigning a casual approach while glancing at my watch, realising I have only three-quarters of an hour.

Cai lifts Chap down from his shelf. 'Okay Pops … here you go … I swear secrecy on Chap's life.'

I reciprocate, moving my mouth towards his ear, where I whisper, 'Something's come up with Miranda and Nathan. I'm not sure what exactly, but they need me straight away. Maybe it's something about Pia. Anyway, I'm heading out soon, and I need you to cover for me until morning.'

'Ooh; mysterious. Well, if Nathan is involved, I trust you. Good luck. Tell you what, I'll leave my phone under my pillow. If you need help, message me.'

'Thanks Cai.'

'Does Rick know, or Mum and Dad?'

'No, just you. Now, I must pack a bag. Relock the front door after me please Cai.'

Cai grunts in agreement, pops Chap back on to the shelf, turns round and continues gaming, while I grab a collection of must-have items, change into my cammo, carry my boots, and creep downstairs in my socks. Without a sound, I exit. I don't continue on my way until I hear Cai, loyally turning the key inside.

12: TARQUIN CEÒLM

'She what!'

'It was last night. She said she went with Miranda and Nathan, but Nathan doesn't know anything about it, and she's not come back.'

'You knew, Cai. You knew, and you didn't tell us.'

'Yes. I'm sorry. It was Chap. It seemed the right thing to do. It was stupid. Mum, I'm worried about her too. I feel terrible about this. What can I do to help?'

'Chap!? You could get her back. Back to Caernef, where she belongs.'

Cai slopes back upstairs, turning on virtuality to drown his guilt. He leans back in the chair and sighs. With automatic gestures, he flicks the controller, hardly seeing the labyrinthine passages through which his hero, a personally designed avatar called Cai, passes. Taking Chap down on to his knee, he mutters to the little cloth doll, *Chap, what can I do?*

Downstairs, Thomas has returned from his morning rounds, opening up the communal areas and checking the site. Maria descends upon him, 'No sign?'

'No sign.'

'That girl is nothing but trouble.'

'She's unpredictable, but she is sound. We need to trust her more.'

Half-hearing his mother's despairing moaning, and then his father's attempt at calming her down, Cai swipes, winces, and tries again. He spots a message, which has popped up in the top right mail box. Disinterested, he clicks on the message, double-takes, and reads it aloud to himself, *Pia requests the presence of Cai at Ceòlm.*

'Mum! Dad! Come and see this.' Cai calls down towards the kitchen. His parents stomp unwillingly up the stairs ducking their heads as they squeeze into the small bedroom.

'Look: a message. It has to be from Poppy. It doesn't make sense.'

'Talk us through it, Cai,' Thomas peers at the screen, speaking in a subdued voice.

'Well, there's no Pia in Future Galactic. The character doesn't exist. There is deliberately no read across between Pia I and the new world. Poppy didn't want it. She wanted Pia to be buried. I'm nearing the finale of Future Galactic. All the virtual world leaders are on the rocket. I just have to find the code. I'm so close. Then this message pops up: *Pia requests the presence of Cai at Ceòlm.'*

'Where the hell is Ceòlm?'

'It's a place in Pia I. Fictional.'

'Cai, darling, that's not going to help us then.'

....

Nathan is distracted. A few nights ago, he inadvertently called Rio *Pia.* She took offence and has returned to her basement flat, where she is stubbornly ignoring his messages. Rio has busied herself with ironing, squeezed up against the blocked-up fireplace; compact living, like so many others, managing in two rooms with basic facilities. Her virtuality wages cover the rent, bills, but no more, and only meagre heating in winter, as Cyber City is in an extortionate area.

It doesn't take her long to clean up. She tidies the lounge, which doubles as a bedroom at night, and the kitchen, only large enough for the basic appliances. Then she sits, weighted down with worries, staring at a blank screen.

…………

Lurking by the lift to the penthouse Handsome spots Nathan rushing in, late. 'Still no word Boss?'

Nathan shrugs, ignoring Handsome, jabbing his identity card at the reader, and disappearing into the penthouse suite.

'I guess the answer is no then.' Handsome says to himself, scrolling down his contacts until he lands on *Rio*, and tries again. But there is still no response; she has phoned in sick, which she has never done before.

So, when Cai phones Nathan, it goes straight to answerphone. He attempts to text, direct message and email, but eventually gives up on Nathan, trying Handsome.

Hi; what's up with Nathan?

The response is immediate; *girlfriend trouble. Face like thunder. Try later!*

Cai returns to virtuality. His online lessons don't start until ten thirty. Half-heartedly, he grabs another half-hours gaming. About to switch over to double maths (virtual), he spots a fresh message and hovers over it, expecting spam.

Pia urgently needs the presence of Cai at Tarquin Ceòlm

Thinking he has read it already, Cai switches over.

…………

It is Robin who exercises more tenacity. In the early afternoon, Maria took Robin's post down to the folly and explained to her how Poppy had disappeared. Robin has been following Miranda's latest machinations with interest, and she suspects her straight away. Knowing she will gain no intelligence from her elusive friend, she is contacting Reginald De Vere, on his antiquated landline. He generally spends his lunchtimes in the drawing room of his baronial pile, skimming a range of actual newspapers, devouring any tasty morsel of left-field news to add to his vast knowledge-base.

'Good afternoon, Reginald!'

'Robin, my favourite girl. How are things with you?'

'Not bad, considering, and you, my old friend?'

'Less of the *old* thank you.'

She imagines his eyes twinkling with mirth, and she retorts, 'We are both getting older …'

'True of every human being my dear. Now what can I do for you?'

'Is Miranda there?'

'Huh! That infuriating strumpet. No. She has not been here for some weeks. She's tied up with her FutureProof, as I guess you know well.'

'She is still on your payroll, Reginald?'

He doesn't answer. Robin hears the turning of the pages of a newspaper, and tries again, 'Reginald, Poppy's missing. I think she has gone somewhere with Miranda.'

'Yes, I know.'

'Oh.'

'I thought you might ring to ask me.'

'And …'

'Robin, my dear, Miranda is a law unto herself. There has been an unexpected hitch in the system. She needs Poppy to reset the programme. It's very unfortunate …'

'There has been a glitch, you mean. Someone is targeting your programme.'

'It's not the Chinese.'

'And we know it's not the Russians.'

'You know I can't possibly discuss it here. I will ask Miranda to deliver Poppy safely back home, if that helps.

Robin sighs, 'Thank you Reginald. That's all I need. You take care now.'

…………

But Poppy does not return by dusk, so Cai has to run down to the folly with Robin's supper.

'Cai! No news then?'

'No. It's all my fault.'

'Rubbish. It's Miranda who is at fault, not you. Come in for a moment, Cai.'

Cai, keen to head home to virtuality, frowns, but

despite being a six-foot teenager, still enjoys boiled sweets from Robin's special tin, so follows her into the kitchen of the folly.

'There are some blackcurrant ones hiding at the bottom.'

He rummages in the tin, finds one for himself, selecting a sherbet lemon for Robin.

'Shall we exchange intelligence?'

'Sure. She left last night after dark. Said she was going with Miranda and Nathan. I locked the door behind her and swore to secrecy, but I thought she would be back. I mean …'

'I don't think Nathan is involved this time.'

'No. I got a message from him early saying as much, but Nathan's having girlfriend trouble and hasn't been answering.'

'Hm. She is with Miranda. That is clear. Maybe she only mentioned Nathan to get you on board.'

'Aargh. I have received a message through virtuality, but I don't understand it.'

'It says …?'

'Something about can I meet Pia at Ceòlm. It just doesn't make sense.'

'Ceòlm; the earth?'

'What?'

'There is an earth called Ceòlm somewhere in the Oxfordshire countryside. I went there with Miranda a few years back.'

Cai throws his arms around Robin's neck, almost toppling her over. 'You got it Robin. You genius. Excuse me if I run back home now. Need to get on to this with Mum and Dad.'

…………

But despite phone calls, and Robin pulling in her close contacts, the community at Ceòlm seems to be a red herring. Poppy's mobile is on permanent answerphone, moreover, the autumn weather is deteriorating, with a combination of thunderstorms and high winds.

....

Rick takes the circuitous bus back from college, appearing to doze under his hood, deciding what to do next. Poppy hasn't appeared at lectures and isn't answering his calls. He considers whether she is side-lining him, but he realises she wouldn't want to miss lessons. It's not about him, he decides, but it is one of her hair-brained save-the-world activities, he is sure. He stomps upstairs, locks himself in his bedroom, and tries contacting her again.

Failing, Rick turns to virtuality in a well-used homework-avoidance technique. Before he even moves his heavily armoured avatar called Piaras, a message pops up: *Pia urgently needs your presence at Tarquin Ceòlm.*

Rick reads and re-reads the message. Surely there is no coincidence that Poppy has gone AWOL and he receives an odd message about Pia. But what the hell is *Tarquin Ceòlm?*

It only takes Rick a few minutes to locate Tarquin, a country club just outside Oxford, but nothing about Ceòlm. The only Ceòlm he knows is in Pia I. He replies to the message, typing clumsily: *The white sea eagle is on his way.*

He grabs his thick faux-leather jacket, his phone, and corners his dad, who is slumped at the kitchen table drinking his favourite cheap imitation Irish Boru to drown his despair at the state of the world. He doesn't even hide the bottle when Rick bursts in.

'Dad, I'm of to the gig now. You remember, with my new girlfriend? I'll be late. Might even sleep over there with a mate. Don't worry about me. Okay?'

'Don't do anything I wouldn't do, Rick my son.' He drawls, smiling inanely.

Rick checks the time on his phone, heading for the bus stop. Not yet seeing the bus rounding the corner by the private store, he darts into the convenience store, grabs some coke, crisps and a pasty, waves his phone over the sensor and makes it to the bus stop just as the X800 draws in.

'Station.'

…………

Rick has never travelled further south than Worcester. His Mum took him there to meet his grandparents, before she died. He was very young; hardly remembers it. This trip is the most exciting thing he has ever done. Peeping above the virtuality screen he sees towns flash by, framed by the edges of his hood, as the Alstom tops 300 kmph. On the lookout for ticket-checkers, he grips his phone. Having only purchased one-way tickets for sections of the journey, he knows he is vulnerable, but be blowed if he is going to use up his bar tips. He might need them later on.

Relieved that he had the sense to choose a seat from Birmingham with a superfast cushion charger, Rick chuckles at his boosted battery. Time goes quicker when you have virtuality. No more messages, but he is determined. After all, Poppy mentioned the place called Tarquin once. She had worked there and used the earnings to buy her books. Rick has an immense memory, but he cannot find any link between Tarquin and Ceòlm. One is in Oxfordshire; a real place. The other is in Pia I; totally virtual. Searches give nothing else at all, so he is working in the dark.

…………

Nobody sees the white-tailed eagle soar above the cliffs at Caernef in the early morning storm. Streaks of yellow sunshine illuminate the saturated cliffs while the majestic bird hunts. A curlew sorts through shoreline debris, washed high on the rocks by the night's tempest.

The pane of old glass in the front window of the arcade has slipped through its sodden wooden frame, and gusts are disturbing Poppy's collections, laid out on the bench inside.

Cai glances across the room at the smooth cover on Poppy's bed. He doesn't even switch on, padding downstairs, through the air thick with the smell of strong coffee, to find his parents, with rings round their eyes.

'No news then.'

'Nothing.'

'She is one of the cleverest people I know. She will be okay,' he says, unconvincingly.

'If she's that clever, she would have told us.' Maria has spent the night trying to enter the thoughts of her first-born. Trying desperately to understand her motives. 'Cai, tell us again exactly what she said to you.'

'She said it was confidential – secret. She said something had come up with Miranda and Nathan. She wasn't sure, but guessed it was about Pia. She implied she would be back by the morning.'

Cai doesn't mention his sister's request for him to turn the key in the door. He feels bad about that too, and doesn't want to re-open the subject with his parents.

A frantic knocking at the back door startles them all. Thomas glances hopefully at Maria before opening up. A massive gust of wind sends ash from the grate up into the air rattling the china on the dresser. A mass of sodden leaves slides on to the doormat.

'Robin! Come in. You might have blown away on a morning like this!'

'To tell the truth, I was worried, and didn't fancy sitting alone down there with my concerns. I thought I might cadge breakfast with you.'

Maria flusters over plates, bread and yet more coffee. Thomas holds his head in his hands, while Robin makes small talk with a monosyllabic Cai.

....

In the penthouse suite overlooking the littered streets of Cyber City, Handsome has managed to persuade Rio to talk with Nathan.

'You called me Pia; Pia, Nathan! How do you think that made me feel?'

'I'm genuinely sorry. Rio, I had been working on Pia all day. She was stuck in my mind. It wasn't about you, or us at all. Please don't overreact.'

'Hang on. Why were you working on Pia when we have moved on to Future Galactic. There shouldn't be any more Pia, right? Either you are lying to me, or you are hiding something. It doesn't look good Nathan.'

Nathan glances at his computer screen, then switches off. Completely off. He stares out of the window at a young woman sitting on a bench eating a takeaway, walks over to the door to his office, and clicks it shut. He draws his chair up close to Rio. She is still seething.

'Well? What have you got to say, Nathan?'

Nathan takes her hands in his, and holds them tightly enough to convey the importance of what he is about to say, but not too tight that she feels he is imposing himself. In a confidential tone, he tries to explain, 'Rio, I love you. I really do. Believe me.'

'So?'

'You know how I feel about Pia. You, especially you, have seen this from deep inside virtuality. Pia is the best creation ever. In a world dogged by fear of the future, of tech, of extinction, of a post-capitalist mess, to put it bluntly, Pia struck a chord deep within the human psyche. My success with virtuality was sort of accidental. I just did what I love to do, but the success of Pia was carefully crafted to the minutest detail, that I am so proud of her. I lived and breathed Pia. She is a part of me. Pia represents all that is good in a corrupt world. She retains her natural simplicity. She is free of the burden of modern living. Pure, but not innocent. Pia still has a part to play Rio.'

'You created Pia at the expense of Poppy, at the expense of your integrity. You promised Poppy you would give her up. And you promised me … that despite your infatuation with a virtual woman, you still had the capacity, the desire, for a real-life relationship with me. I believed you. Yet you persist with *her*.'

'Yes. You are right I messed up with Poppy, but I will make it up to her. I will show you. It's just … I can't explain.'

'Why ever not?' Rio hisses.

Nathan's success in calming her wrath is limited. He tries again, 'Rio, you need to ask Miranda. I'm not at liberty to say stuff, not to you or to anyone.'

'That witch Miranda has you under her little finger Nathan. I'm not at all sure I support Miranda in what she is doing in such secrecy. Robin, that's another matter completely. Robin's vision for the future is strong, fair and unwavering. If we can use #FutureProof to gain more and more followers, if we can continue to mobilise the runners and the earths. If we can excite the younger generation, it might not be too late. Poppy knows that. I know that, and I think you know it too.'

'I do, but …'

'Nathan, years ago you were part of #Spoiler, like me. You saw how the power of many once insignificant people made a massive difference. We shifted the future trajectory of the planet. You saw it.'

'I know. #Spoiler was an amazing success. But then what happened, eh? It fizzled out because those with power found other ways to control us. Now, ten years later, world politics is more fragile than ever, the natural world is going downhill rapidly, the atmosphere, the climate. We have to act quickly and decisively. Robin's motivational speeches and loyal army will not be enough Rio; you know it.'

'Well, I'm sorry Nathan, but until you can be open with me, I'll be taking a back seat in your personal life. Give me space will you. I have work to complete on Future Galactic. There's no Pia in it at all, and that's flat. Pia is old news.'

'But Rio …'

She turns towards him fondly, finding it hard to stand her ground, 'Let's have a breather and talk again later. You look like you need a coffee Nathan my dear.'

…………

Nathan hurries out of the building, telling Handsome he will not be back until tomorrow. He wants to travel alone, and incognito, so hires a car, tapping the postcode for Tarquin into the autonomous sat nav.

…………

Rio's split-second decision to grab her bag and raincoat, and to follow him, at a distance, on foot, means she is unable to go any further than the car-hire depot, but Rio has performed many acts of kindness for runners over the years, and she knows exactly who to call in at this point.

Stepping over a heap of discarded pizza boxes on the pavement, greasy from remnants of cheese, she stands with her back to the 24-hour fast food joint, peering through the windscreen of the hire car. Seeing Nathan set the auto sat nav, she makes a call. 'I don't mind who; anyone in the area? A runner – an ecocar, even better. Yes, I have the registration.'

The ecocar draws up outside the takeaway within a couple of minutes. Rio grabbed two coffees and a bag of mini-bites from the vending machine, while she was waiting. As she opens the passenger door, she hands the eco-cups into the interior, she says, 'Thanks Troy; he took the Oxford Road. Greenerwheels hire car reg CC34 HTN.'

13: PROGRAMMERS

I don't leave until I hear Cai, loyally turning the front door key inside. A storm is brewing, and as I run down the path to the arcade, effectively blindfold, I feel the chill breeze on my cheeks, and imagine bats flitting across my route. Wrangling with a desire to turn back, I fear Miranda is still in the arcade, but find my precious and peculiar shed sitting quietly in complete darkness on the clifftop.

I unlock, and creep inside with caution, locate the package containing Miranda's discarded phone, in its hiding place, and stash it in the zip pocket of my bag, along with my penknife, placing Rio's Pia hologram in my trouser pocket, for good luck. I sling Nathan's whin necklace over my head. I need all the good luck charms at my disposal tonight.

Thank goodness Miranda didn't think to look for her phone. I need a better hiding place. As I am leaving, hurriedly, Arcadian B, abandoned by Miranda on my work bench, sparkles in my torchlight. 'You're coming too Arcadian,' I whisper, stashing my treasure in my bag. I lock up and leg it towards the station.

It takes slightly longer than I planned, due to the darkness, and the need to take a convoluted route to avoid the night-time patrols at the entrance to Caernef. I plunge through the undergrowth of the copse, anxious at the cacophony of rustling, climb over the five-bar gate, then into the field of sheep. Their eyes are glowing and I can hear the munching of grass as I skirt the field under cover of the hedge. Pausing at a spot only I will recognise, I slice a phone-sized rectangle of turf, then dig with the broad blade of my pocket knife. I place the mobile under the sod and press it down with my boot, slide the knife into my bag, and continue along the hedgerow, counting my footsteps, and stepping cautiously over the stile on to the lane. I am nearly opposite the station.

Fearful that I have missed her, as she is an impatient type, and will not wait longer than necessary, I stand still and silent, all my senses alert. The short platform is in darkness. A branch cracks in the wind, and a flurry of pinecones scatters on the forecourt. There is a car, not at the station, but in a scuffed pull-in just down the lane. I move silently back into the field and make my way down the hedgerow, pausing right by the car, shielded by the mass of hawthorn. Miranda is on the phone, and she is alone. I can discern the rise and fall of her voice. My heart misses a beat. This is it then. Back on to the tarmac, I reveal myself. Headlights followed by the click of the passenger door.

'Good.'

'I'm not convinced, Miranda.'

'But you came, and you were just on time. Classy.'

'I haven't brought much with me.'

'I only need your finger tip. You don't need anything else.'

'Not that again.'

'Poppy, I must warn you, I am employed by Reginald De Vere. Reginald provides the transport. He ensures he is kept informed. What I mean is, that there is a possibility Reginald will be monitoring our conversation. I just wanted you to know.'

'Okay. You have more to risk than me, I guess.'

'Bravado might get you into trouble. I'm saying be careful. This is far more serious than you know. We need to drive to Tarquin now. I will explain to you while we travel. Are you okay with that?'

'Yes.'

The car starts automatically with a virtually imperceptible hum.

'Blimey, Miranda, how did you do that?'

'Universal micro implant – no need for a card or a power button.'

'Cool. Universal?'

'Works for most cars. Can be useful.'

'Is it legal?'

'Not technically, but; well, it's authorised.'

'Ooh.' Flatter her and gain as much intel as I can. She drives fast. Very fast, which is both exhilarating and alarming. The roads are relatively empty at this hour.

'So, Poppy Kiwan, it's time you understood.'

'#FutureProof?'

'Yes. Listen carefully. You may only get to hear this once.'

'I'm listening Miranda.'

'I want to take you back a bit. You remember #Spoiler?

Tempted to take Miranda back even further to my memories of her cavorting with the enemy at Caernef when I was hiding in the vegetable shed, but now is obviously not the time, so I simply say, 'Yes.'

'There was a period; one term, that is four years or so, of stable and ethical government. But it gave the establishment time to regroup. The country was effectively bankrupt, wars broke out in hotspots across the world and people were frightened. Robin's courageous initiative faltered. Despots tightened their control overseas, and the country returned to the grip of the right, where it has been ever since. You with me?'

'I am, but this is well-known. What's so secret?'

'My #FutureProof is far more than an ethical attempt to incite a grassroots uprising. That's been done, and it only worked in the very short term. I've always believed in Year Zero, since I started working for Reginald fifteen years ago. Draw a line and start again. It's the only way.'

I remember Dad talking of Year Zero way back; a baddie called Karl dreamt it up. It's what led to #stoptheglitch. I know more about this than she thinks.

'That's what Karl used to say.'

Silence.

'Miranda?'

'What do *you* know about *him*?'

'Only that Year Zero was his obsession, and he came to Caernef once.'

'God. Thought that had drifted into the sands of time.'

'Sorry?'

'Poppy, forget about Karl. He died long ago. Ideas of Year Zero did start when *they* played their #stoptheglitch games. But here and now, the reality is that humanity has gone downhill since then. There are too many dangerous maverick extremists out there, leading countries, leading movements.'

'I met Tod Humboldt at Caernef Miranda.'

'Good God! You did. Before he …'

'Robin says mavericks are to be celebrated.'

'She does. Maverick eccentrics like her, and ethical political rebels maybe, but Robin would definitely agree with me that our current war is with *dangerous* maverick extremists. Thank goodness; here's the A5.'

As the route becomes straighter and wider, Miranda drives even faster. I consider whether Robin would agree with Miranda. I try to imagine who Miranda is alluding to, and what she intends to do about it.

'I'm hoping to hear what you are doing about these dangerous people.'

'Two options: leave the world behind to wallow in the slough created by centuries of human short-term thinking, or provide all the despots with an offer they can't refuse.'

'The trip to the future. The Clinician, the Scurrilous were talking about it. I remember; there was a seat for Reginald.'

'Yes.'

'And?'

'Last week, the plans were hacked. We had to take them all down and will rebuild from scratch. We can do that, but we need your fingerprint, Poppy.'

'Why me, and why my fingerprint, Miranda?'

'You, because you are the child of Caernef, and Pia is your alter-ego. Your finger print because the committee decided it. You mustn't know any more than this. The whole thing only works if you are innocent, do you see?'

'Not really. It feels as if, like with Pia, I am being taken advantage of, if you ask me.'

'The opposite entirely.'

I'm feeling very uncomfortable about this. I don't want to cooperate, but I need to play along at this stage. 'So, my finger print is the real human trigger, but what about Pia? How does my finger link with virtuality. There is a link, right?'

'You're sharp.'

'Miranda?'

'Nathan is working on that aspect. All is in hand. Anyway, Poppy, we are heading for Tarquin. The committee is meeting soon, to discuss our strategy following the hack. They have asked me to refresh your fingerprint.'

'So, all I have to do is to put my finger on the reader again.'

'Yes.'

'But this time, you are not going to drug me, or trick me, it's all above board?'

'The committee wants you to *understand* the importance of your role.'

She's lost me now. It's like they are making it look more complicated than it is. Well, that's not winning me over. On the motorways now, we sail round Birmingham in an uneasy silence.

'I will be back home tomorrow, won't I? Otherwise,

they will be worried. Cai can only cover for me for so long Miranda.'

'We will get you back Poppy.'

I'm not convinced, and take my phone out of my bag. With a squeal of brakes, Miranda pulls over on to the hard shoulder. She not only demands my phone, putting it in her jacket pocket, but takes my bag, and secures it in the boot. Having stolen my only means to escape, as well as Arcadian B, she accelerates back on to the M40, guarding me, her prisoner.

'What was all that about?'

'Can't take the risk.'

I regret my decision to join her on this wild goose chase, but, I reflect, she didn't give me a lot of choice. She would have come back for me if I hadn't joined her, I know it.

'Miranda, I didn't choose to live at Caernef. I didn't choose to be the innocent girl who provides a fingerprint for the ride to the future. I didn't choose any of this, and you tell me to have *agency*.'

'Calm down, Poppy. It's actually simple. Your fingerprint will activate the rocket. Only yours. We need you there, with the equipment.'

'The rocket, eh? And then I will be free to go, with my belongings?'

'Of course.'

'You know, some days, I wish I never got caught up with you at all.' I mumble, regretting this, as soon the words have burst out of my mouth.

Signs for our exit from the motorway. Miranda constantly checking the time. Nearly midnight. Familiar roads leading us to Tarquin. I wish I was seeing the place again in different circumstances. The building is largely in darkness. Mixed feelings as we skid on the gravel, triggering security lights. We exit the car and she ushers me through into the Tarquin conservatory. Down the all too familiar stairs, past the scribbled notice 'Earthworks'.

'Earthworks is compromised,' she says, taking me down more steps. Lights flick on automatically as we descend. On my best behaviour, I do not protest. Another sheet of paper, pinned hastily to a heavy door. This time the scrawl says *Ceòlm.*

'Oh! Ceòlm!'

'You know it, Poppy?'

'It's in Pia I. The Castle of Ceòlm.'

'Nathan named it. Come on in.'

....

A much smaller room under Tarquin; cramped and damp. Whitewashed walls, two women busy working at computer desks, surrounded by heaps of tech equipment. Quite a contrast to virtuality, where everything is spotless and organised.

'Took your time,' a voice from the far side of the room. A man who I have not seen before. A touch disrespectful towards Miranda.

'We came as quickly as humanly possible,' she retorts, turning to me, and explaining, 'These two programmers are rebuilding the whole system. They need to replicate your fingerprint. That's why we've come all this way. Nobody else is to know about this. Not Cai, not your parents, nor any boyfriends or prying hangers on. You understand, don't you?'

'So, this is the girl,' the disrespectful man observes.

Miranda feels me bristle. 'Poppy, this is my colleague, Hans. He is in charge of the rebuild.'

I can see the digital pad where they will press my finger. Miranda grabs my right hand. She has forgotten I'm left-handed. For someone so scrupulous, she makes uncharacteristic errors. I go along with it, press my right forefinger on to the pad. The technician nods. I reclaim my finger.

'That's done that then.' I observe wearily, expecting to head home.

'Not so hasty,' drawls Hans, adding, 'Miranda, leave the

girl with me now. I'll make sure she is safe, like we agreed.'

I begin to worry. Miranda yawns, then checks the time. She tells Hans that she is handing over responsibility to him, and addresses me, 'Don't worry, Poppy, it will be fine. Thank you for doing this today. You might manage to save the world after all. See you soon.'

Before I can protest, she leaves, glaring at Hans, and smiling at me. Snake. How many times have I said I will never trust her again. So, I find myself forcibly shut in this accursed cramped workroom, deep under Tarquin, and I realise Miranda still has my bag, my phone, as well as any chance I have of freedom. All I am left with is my raincoat, with the hologram of Pia, given to me by Rio at virtuality, deep in my pocket.

'I see what Nathan liked about you,' Hans sneers, and he, too, leaves, slamming the door, muttering about getting some sleep and seeing me in the morning. The two programmers continue tapping, ignoring me. I sit gingerly on Hans's swivel chair and study their movements. They are obviously under pressure to achieve their tasks at speed. No interactions. Totally focused on their work. I remain silent. Blend into the background while time passes so slowly.

After an hour or so, one of the women takes off her headset, nudges the shoulder of her colleague, and they both get up off their chairs, stretching. To my dismay, they collect their shoulder bags from a hook on the back of the door, and leave. One retrieves what I guess is a packet of cigarettes.

While they are gone, I leap into action, without a care for consequences, place myself at the open screen of the right-hand computer. I familiarise myself as best I can, search for virtuality, which seems to be on open login, enter and type frantically: *Pia requests the presence of Cai at Ceòlm.* Attempt to send it to Cai. Not sure whether it actually sent. Reflecting that he needs to know where I am, I send a second message: *Pia urgently needs the presence of Cai at Tarquin Ceòlm*. Hope it's sufficiently obtuse not to attract attention. No sound of the programmers returning, so I send a similar message to Piaras, the name of Rick's avatar. You never know, he might see it and think to contact Cai. I close virtuality just in time, as the screen-lock kicks in. That was close.

Sitting on Hans' chair again, I feign sleep, so that once the two women return, they might not suspect anything. Feet on the stairs, door opens, and immediately I can smell the reek of cigarette smoke. They speak to each other in a language that I don't understand, don the headsets, and resume their work. Not sure what I have landed in here. It's uncomfortable, and I manage no sleep other than a couple of fitful dozes.

....

After interminable hours, I am dragged back to reality by the clatter of heavy steps on the stairs and the burst of an opening door. I leap up, aware Hans has returned, and he might not take kindly to me occupying his chair.

'Ah, Poppy. Sorry if I was unwelcoming yesterday. It had been a long and difficult day. No excuse, I know. Here; breakfast.' He thrusts a paper bag, emblazoned with the Tarquin crest, into my hands, and gets one of the women to organise mugs of tea for us, from a kettle plugged in behind them. This is a very makeshift operation. It's hard to believe that Miranda is planning to restore Year Zero using such crudely improvised facilities.

In the absence of a spare chair, I stand, devour the fresh croissant, which smells sweet and almondy like the Tarquin kitchens, and sip my tea.

'Now, Poppy my dear, we have some questions to ask you before you head for home. This thing needs to be squeaky clean. Won't take long, but I need Miranda, oh, and Reginald. He's arriving this afternoon, so you'll have to wait.'

'Beatte, take Poppy up to the facilities, and then deliver her to Miranda, once she arrives. She will know what to do with her until this afternoon.' Turning towards the wall, he mutters to himself, 'What a mess. What a bloody mess.'

I swig the dregs of the tea, zip up my coat, secretly hold my Pia hologram in my pocket, for good luck, and present myself silently to Beatte. With an impassive face, she leads me up the stairs, across the conservatory to the female staff toilets. I know these toilets well, so choose the only cubicle that I remember has a window. Just hope I am able to squeeze out of it.

After using the toilet, I gently push the metal catch, opening the frosted window wide. Yes. I flush, in an attempt to mask the sound of my exit, scramble up like a cat, easing myself through, and dropping down, thankfully unseen, on to the gravel. Burdock burrs. Run. Be Miranda. Be Pia. Be me. Speed across the rough ground behind the rambling outbuildings at the back of Tarquin and hurtle over a fence, clumsy in my desperation, catching my coat on a hook or something. Crouch down and scan the area. A huge metal barn in the adjoining field. What would Miranda do? Hide in plain sight. Climb. Advantage of height while I gather my thoughts.

So, I sidle up to the massive barn doorway, checking in all directions. Once inside, amidst the clutter of agricultural machinery, I see the ideal place, up on a platform where farming implements and sacks are stored. A sort of barn mezzanine. I'm used to heights, from the Caernef cliffs, so am not at all daunted, as I balance on the rungs of the access ladder, gain my footing on the metal platform, and gaze down at the area below.

Come on Poppy. You need to be astute. You need to beat that slippery Miranda at her own game. My heart beats loudly in my chest. My hands shake. I breathe long and slow, taking in my surroundings. Don't want to be cornered up here. The ladder is the only access, but having committed, I will stay here for a while. If only I still had my belongings, and, of course, a phone. I settle down on some sacks in a position that allows me a full view of the entrance door.

They seem to be in a right pickle about this trip to the future. I really disliked Hans. And what does, *earthworks has been compromised,* mean exactly? I want nothing more to do with any of it. Ha! Fancy Miranda taking my right hand. Last time it was my left. They will never achieve their half-baked Year Zero plans with clumsy errors like that. I guess Hans is in charge of assembling the guest list, like Miranda said, to blast off, leaving the doomed world behind. I wonder where they will go, the select few, who think they are better than the rest of us, and who want to use me to protect themselves from any blame. Despicable.

I decide my first priority is to escape from Miranda's clutches. I should have listened to Robin. Hans and Miranda will assume I am heading well-away from Tarquin, which is a good enough reason to stay here a while. Also, the weather is pretty rough. My second priority must be to let Cai, Mum and Dad know I am safe. That is, if I am safe. But I am suddenly overcome with an all-consuming weariness. Fighting against my eyes closing …

14: HIGHER AYNHO

I must have slept for hours, my fingers clasped around the Pia hologram in my coat pocket. Along with my whin necklace, the only tangible tokens of who I am, and why I am here. Fortunately, Miranda didn't take my watch from me, either. People don't wear watches much these days, because they have their phones. It's three o'clock, and there's an afternoon storm brewing. The triangle of sky that is visible out of the doorway, is ominously dark. The wind is echoing in the metal panels of the barn. Before I have time to properly wake up, there is a hammering of heavy rain on the roof. Suddenly, two figures dash into the barn, and cower behind the enormous combine. At least they won't hear me through the din of the rain. I duck down on to my belly to watch. They are nervous, and keep glancing out of the doorway. Definitely not farmers or locals out for a stroll getting caught by the weather; they seem to be hiding, like me. Must be to do with Tarquin. Must be after me …

I fix my gaze on their faces.

What the … it's Rick. My Rick. Or someone who is very like him. It can't be? Surely? I just manage to stop myself calling out, wary of the woman who is with him. Is this a dream? Rick is at Tarquin with a woman. He never said. He must be in with them. He's a plant. Perhaps I'm over-sensitive and it isn't Rick at all. Anyway, who is that woman? It's not Miranda, or Beatte. She is curvy, bundled up in a large raincoat. She stays apart from Rick as if she doesn't know him well. I hold my breath and stare at her, willing her to take down her rain hood.

The woman shakes the drips off her head, like a dog, throwing her hood down. She half-turns towards me, revealing her face, but not looking upwards.

Now I know her too. It's got to be Rio; my friend Rio from Nathan's virtuality. What on earth is she doing here? What the hell is she doing with Rick? They don't even know each other, at least, that is what I thought.

It's obvious; they are looking for me at Tarquin. They must be. But nervous this is a trap; I remain silent a while longer. I don't want them to leave without seeing me. The rain hammers down. Rick spots the ladder, indicates to Rio. She is not very fit, I know that. She shakes her head. He seems disgruntled, and moves towards the ladder himself, but at that very moment, three dogs dash into the barn, growling ominously, followed by three men. Are they simply seeking shelter? The farmer perhaps. No, they are not seeking shelter, *they* are … looking for me. Dogs growl, sniffing around the combine.

Rick and Rio have disappeared.

It is like a scene from virtuality playing before my eyes. I long to control it. If I was Cai, I wouldn't hesitate, shooting the dogs, restraining the three men, uniting myself with Rick and Rio. But the reality of the situation hits home. It is the men who are armed, and this is no imaginary palliative to real life. I lie frozen to the spot, fearing the worst.

The men begin to search the floor around the machinery. The dogs are baying by the combine, their yelps rising and falling above the beating of the rain.

As they turn towards the ladder, I recognise Hans, but before I have time to squirm to the back of the platform, Rick walks out from behind the combine with his hands above his head.

No Rick, no! A voice screams inside my head. This must

be all my fault. He is here because of me, and his life is in danger. Yet I cannot intervene; not prepared to relinquish my freedom. I refuse to sacrifice myself to that scheming Hans.

The dogs calm down, having secured a prisoner. The men surround Rick. Hans throws Rick's hood back and grabs his arms, snapping a restraint on his wrists. Indistinct voices. No attempt to search further. They exit. With Rick.

I blink back confused tears, rub my eyes with my sleeve, trying to see Rio below. I fix my gaze on the doorway, determined to spot immediately if Hans returns, or if Rio sneaks out.

The rain continues to beat down while the wind threatens to lift sections of roof. The sky darkens further. For what seems an eternity, I keep still, my eyes silently locked on the doorway.

As the evening rolls in, the darkness in the barn intensifies. I can sometimes glimpse a flash of bluish light out on the far side of the cab of the combine. It comes and goes. Not security or a fixed light, but more likely to be a phone. Rio's phone.

Between bouts of complete paranoia, and nursing cramp, I conclude that Rio must be friend rather than foe, despite her allegiance with Nathan. As the bluish light is still flickering sporadically, I decide to move. It's worth the risk, otherwise I will be stuck here all night, alone so close to my adversaries. Vulnerable. I crave a glimpse of Rio's smile. Her reassuring voice; *it's alright, Poppy, it's all going to be fine.*

But Rio moves first. She emerges from her hiding place and heads for the doorway. I act impulsively, throw the hologram down towards her. A brittle clatter in the dark void of the barn. She startles. I lie low. Don't think it broke. She scans the cement floor with her phone, and looks as if she is about to give up, when she spots Pia's beautiful face, glinting in the gutter. She pounces. Picks Pia up, stands with her back to the cold metal wall, and looks upwards.

The metal bars of the ladder are chill to my touch as I descend quickly. I reach Rio.

'Poppy! Thank goodness! How long have you been up there?'

'Rio! What are you doing … with Rick?' I whisper.

'It's not safe here. We must move, and quickly. Stay together. You follow my lead. I know where to go to reach safety.'

Rio grabs my hand in hers. She had the sense to wear gloves on this chill night. Always practical. I follow her, blind and silent, still not completely confident that this isn't a trap, but left with few options.

Rio leads me out of the barn, past the back of a sleeping Tarquin, on to a rough track. We walk rapidly without speaking, setting a distance between us and that den of thieves and murderers.

'Why, Rio? How?'

'Not yet. Keep walking.'

We skirt a couple of fields bereft of wildlife. No moon, and intermittent squally rain. Finally, she draws me close behind the huge trunk of an oak, puts her finger to her lips to signal silence, and taps rapidly on her phone.

'Telling your mum you're safe. And … I've got a geolocation at last. There's a lane directly to the north. I'm being transported by a friendly runner called Troy. He's been waiting for me to contact him.' She taps again. 'Troy will pick us up. He knows of an earth not far from here, and will take us there. A place of safety. Then we can talk.'

Dumbfounded by her control of the situation, I acquiesce. We cover the ground quickly, heading for the dimmed headlights on the lane. While I scramble into the back of the ecocar, Rio passes something to me, all scrumpled up. It is the scarf I gave her at virtuality. My scarf. I wrap it round my neck, soft and warm. It smells of Rio now, a faint scent of her perfume.

Troy, who is not wearing the sleek silver runner clothes

I remember, talks with Rio. She thanks him profusely, explaining she is going to drop me at the earth, they will stop briefly, and then she needs to return to Tarquin.

'To Tarquin? Rio, are you mad?' I blurt out from the back seat.

'We need to know what is going on,' she replies, turning back to Troy, and checking with him that the earth is still as good as she remembers. He knows it well, and reassures her. I start shivering. The enormity of this is coming over me. So much for Rick's comment that I am a small person without any influence. I am caught up in something huge.

'Why was Rick with you Rio?' I want answers, now, but she tells me to wait.

We pull on to an access road to a farm, and the ecocar bounces over potholes. I have only visited a couple of earths. They are always well-hidden off the beaten track, even in populated areas. Ingenious.

Troy talks to Rio, 'That's as far as I can go Rio. I'll wait here for you. No hurry. I'll grab a kip. But I'm on duty back in the capital in the morning. Don't be too long.'

We emerge into the night, ominous clouds against a full moon, and a buffeting wind, which brings bursts of heavy rain. Hoods up, we talk as we walk.

'Thank you, Rio. You saved me. But I don't understand.'

'First things first.'

'What?'

'Here, Poppy, take my phone and talk to your mum. Tell her you are with me and you're safe. Try not to talk too much. Just reassure her, yes?'

I take Rio's phone and dial Mum's mobile number. She picks up straight away. Anxious voice, not angry.

'Rio?'

'Mum, it's me. It's Poppy. I'm safe with Rio. All fine. You get some sleep now.'

'Poppy. Thank goodness.' She sobs.

'Try not to worry, Mum, and don't be hard on Cai. He helped me. I asked him. It's not his fault.'

'Yes. Yes. What happened?'

'I can't go into it now. We're in a field on the way to a safe place. It's raining, and we are soaked.'

'Oh. I see. Call again when you can. Stay with Rio. Cai knows her; says she's trustworthy. Take care Poppy. I love you.'

'I love you too, Mum.' Nearly tears in my eyes too. 'Thanks Rio.'

'That's okay. Now; let's talk while we walk. No listening ears or cameras out here in the open air.'

'Where are you taking me?'

'See over there, those lights on the horizon; that's an earth called Higher Aynho. I haven't been there in person, but it's one of the best. We worked with them loads when I was in charge of the midland runners. Their elected leader these days is a young woman called Elfrida. She knows Robin well. She will provide you with a home as long as you need it, and will get you hooked back into your college courses. Remotely. She doesn't need to know more than she does, that you are from Caernef and are in danger. She probably guesses more, but she's discreet.'

'Okay, but why can't I just go home? Am I actually in danger?'

'Look, Poppy, I don't know. I'm as much in the dark as you are, but right now, something's brewing. Miranda and Nathan are collaborating. I don't know whether it's a dastardly plot or a beneficent act to save the world. I just don't know, but I mean to find out.'

We stumble on along the path, worn smooth by the feet of runners. 'Why were you at Tarquin, Rio?'

'Nathan and I had an argument. He left for Tarquin. I don't know why, and I intend to find out. What do *you* know, Poppy?'

I hesitate. Not sure what I can and can't say these days. I opt for simplicity and honesty, 'Miranda came to

Caernef. She is deep into some secret plot for the future and needed my involvement. She took me to Tarquin, but I didn't trust the people there. It felt wrong, so I slipped out of the toilet window.'

Rio laughs. 'Here we are discussing matters of life and death, and you tell me you climbed out of a toilet window. Poppy, you are living your life more and more like Pia.'

'Rio, Pia *is* involved in all of this.'

'I know. That was what Nathan and I argued about. He is still working on Pia, but he said he wouldn't. He told you he wouldn't.'

'And Rick?' We are approaching the gates of the earth.

'Rick got some message from Pia. He thought it was you, and you needed help. He said he was on a rescue mission called white sea eagle. Do you know anything about that?'

'No! Yes! I'm not sure. I did try to send him a message. We did see the white-tailed eagle. Good for Rick. He was coming to help me. That takes courage.'

'Or naivety. Now he's in their clutches.'

'You will go back there, Rio. Get him out too, somehow?'

'Do my best. Now, you will find the messaging is totally different in the earth. They don't work with the outside world in the same way as Caernef does. You will be able to receive messages through Elfrida. It's controlled.'

'So the bastions of free speech and rebellion censor their citizens.'

There is no time for Rio to answer, as we reach a wooden stockade, which delineates the earth from the surrounding agricultural land. Rio reaches up, pulling a rope on the gate post. This is medieval. Two guards appear. One of them recognises Rio from #Spoiler, long ago, and they chat openly about Caernef, Robin and the runners. We are taken into a modest guardroom. Reminds me of the house made of sticks in the three little pigs.

They are very polite to me, but frisk me all over, scanning me for metal items, finding only my watch, and my necklace. Rio has left her belongings in the ecocar.

'Poppy, I must leave now. They will take you to Elfrida. Enjoy your time here. Respect their way of life. This is a refuge, and you are a guest.'

We hug each other tightly. 'Stay safe Rio, and thank you.' I call softly.

....

Elfrida is even younger than I was expecting, and not at all like a mysterious elf queen. Short, stocky, in jeans and boots, with cropped hair. She cannot be much older than me. Our ten-minute welcome conversation started with questions; what do I most value, who do I most admire, and which personal commodities could I not do without. No paperwork, not even digital. I seemed to pass their tests, so she shared a bit about herself.

She has lived here in Higher Aynho since it was set up, a decade ago, when she came here with her parents from way up north. She told me how she was elected as the leader here, where equity is the expectation. She is on a level with all the residents, she explained, and said I would be too. She showed me to my private bunk area in a long stone bothy, presumably once a barn. The other occupants were quietly turning in for the night, so I tried to remain unobtrusive.

Elfrida provided me with stuff for washing, spare clothes, and a map of the layout of Higher Aynho, printed by hand, as well as pencils and a pad of paper. She promised I could use the learning domes every day, and would be able to access my college studies remotely. It seems like weeks ago that I was so excited about starting the module on ecoculture, but it was only the day before yesterday.

Despite my mind buzzing with the strangeness of my new resting place, my bizarre glimpse of Rick, and Rio shining through for me, I sleep.

....

My bunk was more comfortable than it looked, with a straw mattress and padded cotton cover, so sleep came easily. Everything is totally zero carbon here. More so than Caernef. A sweet smell of summer hay seeped out from the pillow. I feel refreshed and curious to explore my new home in the daylight. I need to find the wash house first, and then breakfast. Apparently I pay for meals through labour. Fortunately, I am well-used to cleaning, domestic duties and office paperwork from Caernef … and Tarquin, so I know I can do this. But hopefully, my time here will be short.

The storm has passed, leaving mud everywhere. There are curious boot washes outside the communal buildings; a splendid notion, which I will take back home with me when I return. We could do with boot washes at Caernef. I spuddle past extensive allotments, past open-air sitting areas with fire pits, just like at Caernef, and covered refuges for when it rains.

Robin has told me all about earths. She claims they proliferated and coordinated as a result of #isolate, alongside relaxed planning laws, and an extensive system of runners. Originally, Robin and her crew obtained considerable sponsorship from ecofirms, like Greenerwheels and even WearenotMcDonald's. It was ingenious, and massively successful for a few years. Earths try to remain below the radar, but they sell locally to cover costs; eggs, honey, fruit, vegetables, bread and carpentry items. Some make woven baskets, others specialise in jewellery, or clothing. All natural, manually crafted and all eco-friendly. So, they sell at a premium. Products from earths are really sought-after, and are not available online.

Apparently, on my first day I am excused *toil*; allocated tasks to help run the earth, while I settle in, so I join a group of other young people at breakfast, and blend in with them before looking for the learning domes.

Strangely, Tarquin, Miranda, fingerprints and trips to

the future seem very far away. I have already relaxed into the slower pace of the earth, where time is our own, and where conspiracies seem to be other people's business. Mum could do with spending some time here. Dad would love it too; the routines, the allotments and the shared purpose.

Past the allotments, there are about a dozen learning domes clustered in a field, built from eco-concrete. Each one can accommodate a maximum of twelve people, and you sit on the floor, although there are chairs for people with less mobility or reduced flexibility. I choose the floor, settle on a large, flat embroidered cushion, and switch on the tablet provided. It displays the welcome screen; *UK Earths non-invasive carbon neutral tech* and I log in with the guest password provided to me by Elfrida. Resting the tablet on a sturdy wooden stand, I get comfy on my cushion.

I have been allocated a *buddy*, a girl more or less my age called Jeanne, with piercings and brightly coloured hair, who keeps coming to check I am alright, which I am. I am able to log straight into my college course, and am just in time to attend a live lecture using a borrowed alias. I can listen but can't post comments. The tutor, who I have met a couple of times, is speaking about his passion for the links between genre in cross-disciplinary twenty-first century art. I didn't manage to read the background, but soon get a hang of what is being said, and take notes with a pencil, which is novel.

There is a shop, to which residents seem accustomed, but it is so alien to any shop I have ever been in, that I resort to watching how others play the game before attempting to obtain a few rudimentary belongings to help me through my stay here. You can clock up credit in return for tasks, as well as promised tasks, but the system is not computerised, so the volunteer shopkeeper, today an older lady with limited eyesight, writes everything down on a pad they call the *ledger*. It wouldn't do to be in a hurry.

All in all, Higher Aynho is a good place for me just now. I am going to keep my head down, make some new friends, and catch up with my college work the best I can. Damn virtuality. Damn Tarquin and damn Miranda.

Rick and Rio are my heroes now.

15: RICK

Sheltering in the Tarquin conservatory, Hans and his accomplices have shed their raincoats, returned the dogs to their cages, and are assessing whether Rick, who they believe is called Tom, is indeed a spy interested in the Tarquin goings on, or whether he is an innocent local teenager who was sheltering from the storm. Rick, of course, claims the latter.

'He's got nothing on him. No phone, no stuff. Just a coat. Looks like he got caught in the rain like he said. Don't want to blow this one out of proportion Hans.'

'Did you check the building. He could have easily left his equipment in there,' Hans growls.

'Well, no. Tell you what, I'll go and check now. Got a bigger torch?'

'There's one behind the desk in reception. In case of power cuts. Meet you back outside.'

While one of the men leaves, presumably for the barn again, Hans heads for the programmers downstairs, anxious about timescale, and the third man returns to Rick, who is tied hand and foot under an awning behind the dog cages. He lights a cigarette, offering one to Rick.

'Want one Tom?'

Rick shakes his head, saying, 'No thanks. Don't smoke.'

Rick, and the man engage in short polite conversation, lapsing into long spells of silence. Rick asks, 'What are we waiting for? My mum'll be wondering where I've got to.

Anyway, what's so secret about this place? Dad came here once for a big wedding do. Just seems an ordinary hotel. Nothing special. Nothing worth tying a bloke up like this.'

So when the search of the barn proves to be fruitless, the two men decide it will cause far less suspicion if Rick is let go.

'Sorry about all this Tom. Mistaken identity and all that. No offence taken I hope?' They untie Rick and shake his hand.

'Nah. I'll be on my way then. See you,' Rick responds, appearing relaxed. He saunters away from Tarquin, down the driveway and on to the road through the drizzle. Car lights reflecting on the puddles. If they try anything funny, he wants it to be in full view of the passing public.

…………

Rick reflects that his chance meeting with Rio behind the outhouses at the back of Tarquin had proved to be lucky. *He* was on the lookout for Poppy. *She* was on the lookout for Nathan. Both Poppy and Nathan are tied into some project led by that Miranda, who Poppy had spoken of many times. Things are starting to come together.

Rick knows exactly where Rio stashed his phone. She explained when he decided to give himself up, to give her the possibility of escape. She seemed very competent, whereas he was floundering. She said he should pretend to be a local lad caught in the rain. That worked. He's free again, but he needs to get to Poppy. Exciting stuff, he thinks.

Doubling back and briskly heading for the large metal barn from the road this time, he scoots straight to the combine, ducks down under the front lights, and feels around. Success! With relief, he grabs his phone and her carrier bag containing his wallet. Rio said they would be there, and thankfully, they were. He spares no time, heads out at speed, marching back on to the road, where he phones Rio.

'Hi, Rio, it's Rick. You okay?'

'Yes. I got Poppy. She's fine. Taken her to the earth like I said.'

'You haven't! Thank you, Rio. You sure she is safe.'

'Yes. You mustn't worry. What about you?'

'I played dumb like you said, and they let me go. Picked up my stuff too. Thanks.'

'Splendid. You will go home now? You have done your bit for her. She knows.'

'I'm getting the hell out of here … somehow. Figure I'll hitch.'

'Good luck.'

Rick smiles, cuts the call, listens for traffic, and heads south across fields. Eventually hitting the A43, he hails each truck that passes, persisting until a huge articulated food lorry pulls over. *Revolutionary Bites*. He climbs in.

'Where you heading mate. I'm only going to the M40 services?'

'That's fine,' he grins, from under his damp hood.

…………

Hans spots Miranda, waltzing into the conservatory with a guest.

'Living it up, I see.' He observes, laconically.

'Afternoon Hans. Not my favourite person. You lost Poppy.'

'Hang on now.'

The two men saunter in. One interrupts, addressing Hans, 'We let him go. Just a local lad.'

Miranda interjects, 'Who? When?'

'Hour or so ago. Found him lurking in that barn out the back.'

'Six-foot, age about sixteen, black stubble, hoodie?'

'Yes, but …'

Miranda swipes through a series of images on her phone, and brandishes one, which she was sent recently, a capture from the security cam at Caernef station. 'Rick. Poppy's *friend*.'

'He was called Tom.'

'I despair.' Miranda storms out, leaving her guest high and dry with the three rogues. Tensions are high in the #FutureProof camp this afternoon.

....

But Poppy does not reappear at Caernef, and Robin's gang are keeping anything they know from Miranda.

....

Rio, meanwhile, is on Nathan's case. From her hiding place behind one of the opulent faux pillars in the Tarquin conservatory, she has overheard the heated exchange, and guesses that Miranda could use some higher quality assistance. Rio has over ten years' experience of managing the communication systems for the runners. Initially from a derelict house in Shropshire, where Miranda was sheltered for a few days back in 2023. Then, more recently, she has been working for Nathan on virtuality, linking the two software platforms, supervising programmers, and dipping into the more sensitive areas personally.

Rio decides that Miranda needs her at this point in her career, and she takes the risk. As Miranda heads for the back door leading to the now infamous Tarquin staircase, Rio reveals herself, and intercepts Miranda.

'Hi Miranda! I'm here with Nathan. Not sure of the quality of your current staff.' She gestures back towards Hans.

'Shit! Rio! Fancy seeing you here. You are right. I could do with your skillset right now.'

....

Nathan saunters down the Tarquin staircase to Miranda's makeshift office, worrying about having upset Rio, unsure of his next step. He taps on the door, and as it opens, he sees Rio, ensconced comfortably in a chair next to Miranda.

'Hi Nathan. You didn't tell me you had the sense to bring Rio with you. Now, I'll order coffee and we three will sort this mess out between us.'

....

Rio listens intently as Miranda and Nathan catch up on the #FutureProof project.

'So, Nathan, I thought I had all my ducks in a row, but this latest fiasco, losing Poppy means I can't explain her role to her. Anyway, the important thing is that we have her digital finger print ready. Hans, for all his ineptness with staff, does have the rebuilding of the programme in hand. What about you?'

'Yep. All in hand with me, too. And with Rio on board, we can manage the programme from our end. Do we have a target date, Miranda?'

None the wiser, Rio waits for more.

'We are going to have to bring it forward, which is possible. Reginald is managing the timing of the real-life event. The invitations will be going out as we speak.'

'He was pleased with my algorithm?'

'Yes. Brilliant! It sorted the world leaders, and the billionaires of course, into my two categories. A few surprises on the despot side. Confidential, of course, but you would be amazed. Libya, Yemen, India. Pakistan. Italy! Not all your Russian hangers on, and Chinese sympathisers.'

'Pleased it worked properly. That's what we wanted, wasn't it?'

'Indeed.'

Rio decides to assert her presence, and, picking up on the mood of the conversation, asks, 'So what do you need me to focus on exactly?'

'Ah yes, I'm coming to that,' Miranda opens the door, receives the tray of coffee accompanied by sumptuous pastries, and checks the girl in the Tarquin catering uniform departs without hanging around outside the door. 'This is being branded the *Trip to the Future.* Nathan is overseeing coverage on Future Galactic, of course. As soon as Hans has the programme back to the point we had reached before the hack, we will be needing a project manager to coordinate all participants. Digitally. Right up your street.'

'Okay. And Pia?'

Nathan interjects, 'Pia is sorted. She's ready. At the moment Poppy places her fingertip on the launch pad, Pia will replicate, live, in Future Galactic. The punters will love it. It will not only divert attention away from the event, but it will provide lasting dual footage; the real and the virtual, hand in hand.'

'Genius Nathan.' Miranda is visibly well-pleased with Nathan's contribution. Rio fights against feeling proud, as she is still unsure, but she holds the trump card. She, and only she, knows how to locate Poppy.

'Now, any questions Nathan, before we get back to work?'

'Will you send an invitation to Robin? I know she's not on the list, but …'

'Already thought of that, and the answer is *yes*.' Miranda responds.

'Good.'

…………

Outside the front entrance of Tarquin, Nathan opens the door of the hire car for Rio to get in. 'Rio, darling, how the hell did you do that?'

'I followed you to the car hire, hitched with a runner, followed you into Tarquin, did a bit of a detour with friends old and new, and hey presto!'

'Why?'

'Because I need to be inside not outside this thing. If you and I are to stick together Nathan, which is what I want; really, then there must be no secrets. Especially where Pia is concerned. I know Pia as well as you do. Remember.'

'But not as well as Poppy does. Hope she's not intending to scupper the whole thing.'

'Yes.'

As Miranda rushes out to her car, running slightly late for her next meeting, she glimpses Nathan kissing Rio in the car park.

…………

Rick, Cai, along with millions of other fans, read the expected announcement:

You, too, can take the virtuality Galactic Trip to the Future!

This much-awaited trip has been confirmed

Simply obtain your unique joining code & log in: Saturday 11th November 11am GMT

On the first floor of virtuality in Cyber City, Rio has Nathan's programmers lined up ready to cope with the demand. Codes have been randomly generated, and are meaningless, to divert attention away from the virtuality key code, not yet revealed.

…………

I'm sitting in the learning dome, muffled up in woollies, as here, where there are no sea breezes, this autumn is damply cold, and heating at Higher Aynho is limited. I have special permission to reply to Cai's message. The system is basic, but it's usable. I'm having more difficulty explaining to my new friends why I am so interested in cyber games, as earths do not approve of them. They are far too busy protecting the planet and keeping alive. Cai has let me know about the launch of the virtuality Galactic Trip to the Future. He's already received his unique code, and is excited. I bet Rick has got his too.

Living in an earth has refocused me on what really matters. Like at home, we spend much of our time outdoors, whatever the weather. There's more communal living here, which is okay for a while, but I'm itching to get back to the privacy of the arcade. My new friends are not like people at college, in the real world; they have time, are kind, and focus on things I also hold dear. There are study groups, research into environmentally friendly practices, lots of arts and crafts. I am managing to keep up with my studies, too. Rio got hold of my books, which has helped. She is checking in with me every few days; says once the noise around the trip to the future has died down, it should be safe for me to return home. I do hope so. Even Mum and Dad don't know where I am. It feels dishonest, although I'm relieved not to be burdened by virtuality and Miranda's #FutureProof. That's not the way I want to live, and at least here, I can be myself.

....

Two days away from the launch. I've settled into daily life in the earth, like I have never been anywhere else. But I want to go home.

I am expecting a visitor. It's a bit hush hush; all being organised by Rio, who has promised it isn't Miranda, or Nathan, or any of their crowd. Elfrida came to give me the news yesterday. She said that permission had been granted for a visitor to come to Higher Aynho, and to spend some time with me. She gave nothing away. I can't imagine Rio would want to compromise my safety here. I have to confess; I am uneasy this morning. I have put on my Caernef cammo, and am due up at the gatehouse in five minutes. Mercifully the weather is idyllic for a change; high clouds with patches of sun, but no rain on the cards.

Time to walk slowly along the track. Morning runners come and go with eclectic loads on their backs, and on trolleys. They bring in supplies, then leave, laden with fruit and vegetables. A new uniform for runners, with wearable solar patches, is being phased in. Only the older runners still wear Robin's magical silver. Times change.

The wooden stockade appears on the horizon, and I am reminded of my arrival so many weeks ago. The gatehouse is busy; produce is being handed over, runners charging to and fro. I wait my turn, then telling the guard that I am here to meet Elfrida's special visitor.

'He's outside. I'll call him in.'

I peer through the gateway, and a hooded chap is sitting on a grassy bank, looking out across the fields. Rick?

He bounds in behind the guard, and spotting me, whisks me up into the air, cheering. Runners turn round, grinning at us. I land on my feet with a bump, genuinely thrilled to see my friend once more; a tangible link with my real life again.

'Rick, it is wonderful to see you. I didn't know who it would be. So much I want to ask you.'

'Yes. Yes. I have never seen an earth before. This is a real treat for me … as well as seeing you, of course.'

We chatter together, about college, about earths, about Cai, the trip to the future and about the white-tailed eagle at Caernef. There is a café bar in the centre of the village, past the bunk house, so I take Rick there, choosing an outdoor table a fair distance from anyone else. 'Coffee?'

'You bet. Black please Poppy.'

'I *know*.'

Not sure how this eco-friendly earth coffee will taste, black, but I return with his, and mine with loads of plant milk.

'It's a bit like Caernef here, but without the sea. There's eco-stuff everywhere, allotments and the same sort of people.'

'I suppose, but without Robin. Anyway, Rick, how did you come to be with Rio outside Tarquin? Tell me. I have been wondering ever since.'

Rick relates the tale of his journey from the far side of Wales, how he didn't know what to do once he reached Tarquin, and how he saw Rio arrive in an ecocar, with a runner. 'He didn't have his runners' costume on, but you can generally tell. I followed Rio as she left him and hid round the back. Thought she was looking for you too, but it turned out she was after Nathan. Anyway, I sidled up behind her. Didn't half make her jump!'

'I saw you with Rio in that huge metal barn. I watched you come out, hands behind your head, to protect Rio. If you hadn't done that, they would have found us both and I would never have been taken safely here.'

I tell Rick he is a hero, but he is modest. I mean, fancy taking off like that all for me. I'm impressed, and I make sure he knows it. We catch up on college; I explain how I have been attending all the lectures, but I can't interact from here. He hadn't realised. Then we move on to discussing Nathan, Pia and virtuality. I'm unwilling to broach the trip to the future, but I think we need to cover it, just to avoid any misunderstandings.

'So, you and Cai have booked your joining codes?'

'Yes, I've got mine safe ready for the day. Cai's finished the game right up to the final scene. I'm catching him up. You can only use the code if you have reached the final scene. It's clever; lures you in.'

'What do you think will happen?'

'Nathan is the only person who knows that,' he says emphatically.

'And Miranda?'

'Really?'

'Rick, listen to me a minute, I think Miranda has a grand plan for a real-life trip. The virtuality one will just be a copy. They are linked. It's so ordinary people can participate too, virtually, while the big guns do it for real.'

'Big guns, eh?'

'I've known this for some time. Miranda is organising a whole load of dignitaries to board a rocket, or a plane, or something. They are going on a trip to … well, to Future Galactic … to start a new civilisation. They want to start from a new Year Zero, start totally again. I think they might be going to get me to press the launch button. Who knows, they might even take me with them. Against my will, of course.

'Fuck. You sure?'

'No. But nearly sure.'

'Is there anything I can do?'

'Well, trouble is Rick, *we are just small people, without influence, without power, and without resource to make any difference at all.*'

'I said that to you before.'

'You did, my friend.'

'Perhaps I was wrong.'

'You know the Caernef train station.'

'Of course.'

'If you walk up the road, towards Caernef, about five metres, not far, and cross over, there is an old wooden stile.'

'What the hell is a stile, Poppy? I wasn't brought up like you, remember.'

'A stile; wooden step so walkers can get in and out of fields without the need for a gate. Look it up online to check. Go over the stile into the field, but stay close to the hedge by the stile. It is a bit prickly from memory. Follow the hedge for a hundred and twenty footsteps. My size feet.' I wave my size four boots at him, quite a bit smaller than his size elevens.

'Okay.'

'There you should see an area of disturbed ground. Same dimensions as a mobile phone. If it's still there, about ten centimetres down, you should find the phone. I buried it for safe keeping.'

'Whose phone Poppy?'

'Miranda's old phone. It might have something on it, you never know.'

'What fun. I'll try to find it and let you know. I'll go tomorrow morning. It's Friday and I will slip out early. Dad will be comatose so he won't ask awkward questions.'

'Thanks Rick.'

'I'm quite good at getting into phones. I'll see what I can do and will let you know. How can I let you know?'

'I can pick up a phone call through Elfrida's office. If you phone this number and ask for me.' I write the number clearly on a scrap of paper from my pocket. Rick types it straight into his phone.

We compost our empty cups and take a slow, thoughtful walk round the stockade, before he has to go. A runner is picking him up at two. As we saunter unwillingly towards the gatehouse, stepping over the molehills, he asks me, 'So, Poppy, would you put your finger on the button? If it sent them off to their fucking Year Zero? Would *you* do it?'

I pause, considering this carefully. 'I don't know. For the moment I'm hoping it will all happen without me. I want to get home, to my collections, to my arcade. I just want to go home.'

'Hah! You see; small lives matter. We'll get you there! Not sure when I'll see you again, but it's been nice today. There's something else before I go.'

'Yes?' I knew they wouldn't arrange this visit unless there was a payback for them.

He lowers his voice, and bends close to my ear. 'They will send for you. On the day. I overheard Rio. They need you to put your finger on the digital launch. It will be done remotely. In Tarquin I reckon. Just thought I'd give you a heads up. I'm not meant to. You understand?'

I nod. 'Are you going to kiss me before you go Rick?'

He bends towards me, shyly kissing my cheek, before disappearing through the gate.

16: TWO ROCKETS

Friday lunchtime. Rick has phoned the communal line, and while I am awaiting the call-back, I am watching three red kites circle above the earth. I miss Caernef. Wonder whether he has found the phone.

'Hi Poppy.'

'Rick.'

'A quick call as I'm on the way home. It was exactly where you said. I'll let you know if I get into it. Okay?'

'Great. Tell you what. I'll phone you from here at five this afternoon. How does that sound?'

'Good. But doesn't give us long. I saw Robin at the station with a group of her oddballs. She looked frail.'

'Oh.'

He rings off, I book a call at five, and continue watching the red kites being bombarded by crows. Robin needs someone who is one hundred percent on her side. The worrying image of her at the station haunts me throughout the day.

....

Unbeknown to Poppy, as she is in hiding, Nathan has called for Cai. It will be such a momentous occasion, and as Cai has been a loyal follower of virtuality since the beginning, Nathan is rewarding him. Cai is sitting proudly beside Nathan on the top floor of virtuality, in the penthouse suite. Four screens surround Nathan's desk, and Cai is gripped.

'All the preparations are going well,' Nathan explains, 'Look; there are the rockets. We can see them for the first time. To think I have funded a trip in them!'

Cai watches the live feed of the launch site on the north of Shetland. The boosters are already standing tall on the two main launchpads, with the capsules on top.

'Can we zoom in Nathan?'

Nathan zooms and the camera reveals the twelve seats in each capsule, with individual viewing windows.

'Cool.'

'We will delay the coverage in virtuality just slightly, so we keep control of content. It won't be totally live.'

'But it will seem live, I mean, how long is the delay?'

'No more than two minutes.'

Cai is impressed. He asks, 'So the guests must be assembling already?'

'The medical examinations are complete. The launch conference is scheduled for this evening, when they will all be briefed, and they will stay in the nearby hotel tonight. Then, we just hope for clear weather in the morning.'

Still inquisitive, Cai asks, 'Why do it in reality too, Nathan?' Why couldn't you just design it in virtuality, and screen it to us all?'

'What difference would that make?'

'Difference?'

'To the world. To the future.'

'You mean, this is for real. This rocket is going to … make a difference. Really.'

'We hope so. But there are so many things that could trip us up. It's ambitious, and fraught with risks. Cyber terrorism for one. The weather for another. Or we get the wrong rocket …'

Cai's eyes open wide as the implications of Nathan's words sink in.'

'Everyone's saying you will bring Pia back, one last time. Are you going to?'

'If I was, would I tell you today young Cai?'

Cai grins, surmising the answer, nevertheless feeling out of his depth. He is not going to let his friend and hero Nathan of the hook, so he persists, 'If you bring back Pia, in virtuality, you will need Poppy for the reality bit, won't you? That's why she is in hiding, ready for the key moment. I get it.'

'I couldn't possibly comment.'

At Nathan's expense, Maria and Thomas have booked into a Night Lodge in Cyber City. They are not going to let Cai out of their sight for long, even though they trust Nathan.

…………

I contact Rick at five o'clock, as agreed, but he has no news. Miranda's phone is not only broken, but heavily encrypted. Rick says it would take a week with skilled hackers to get in. The only thing he can offer me is that, when he opened the back, a slip of paper fell out. On it is written #STG 49909-008. He read the number out to me twice, but I knew it already. It's the same as the number I saw on the scrap of paper in virtuality, when I was working on Pia III with Rio. It's the code that Robin told me was Nathan's incorrect guess for Todd Humboldt's digital casket. The one to stop the glitch. I know now, that *Robin* had the correct code: *peekaboo.*

I thank Rick. He is a good sort, after all. Loyal as well as keen. Then I ask where I might find Elfrida, and I am sent down to the café bar, where she is sitting chatting with a group of young people. When she sees me, she rises and comes over.

'Poppy, I thought I would see you today. You do know …' her words tail off with a hint of regret.

'I guessed.'

'A car will be arriving for you early tomorrow morning. At six, I am told. It has been an honour having you here at Higher Aynho. You will be welcome to return anytime. In fact, I hope you do come back, but of your own volition next time.'

'Thank you, Elfrida. This is the first earth where I have stayed; it has been a complete pleasure. I feel very … nurtured, and sort of clean again. What you are doing here is inspirational. If only more people understood. The natural world needs us to exercise the restraint and care, which I have experienced here.'

'It's like Caernef?'

'Yes, Elfrida, it is very like Caernef.'

She smiles with pride. 'Say hello to Robin for me tomorrow, if you see her.'

'Robin? She will be there?'

'Oh, I had assumed. I mean, it will be such a triumphant day.'

'Will it?'

'Of course. #Futureproof. You know?' She shakes my hand, and returns to her meeting, while I am left questioning all my suspicions.

…………

I'm up before dawn, having already placed all the belongings loaned to me in Higher Aynho on the bedside cabinet by my bunk. I washed and wrapped the scarf, which I gave to Rio, which she returned to me, and left it for Elfrida.

Now I'm in my cammo, washed fresh, and boots. Empty pockets, and overflowing thoughts. I pause as I walk down to the gatehouse, gazing across the rolling fields, recently ploughed by the team of Clydesdales; beautiful heavy horses who live here at the earth. The breeze carries with it a whiff of agriculture, like at home. One breath it is pleasantly sweet, and next breath it tips into rotting vegetation. I have felt at home here. The temptation is to stay, to refuse to go, to hide, or to feign some sort of illness or injury to prevent me doing whatever I seem destined to do later today.

I am still unsure whether #FutureProof is a panacea or a curse. Worrying about this, I thank the guard, turn my back on Higher Aynho, and squeeze into the ecocar, which is driven by a runner in silver, accompanied by a woman who I have never seen before. I guess he has a persuasive chaperone in case I prove awkward. And there, on the dash, is my bag, containing my phone. My belongings taken by Miranda. I grab them, and cling on to my old things.

It is no surprise to me when we take the all-too-familiar road to Tarquin. And there on the forecourt, is Rio, smiling.

'It will be okay, Poppy. Trust me.'

In a daze, after weeks spent away from reality, I follow her silently, down the Tarquin staircase. The very location fills me with fear, but Rio's chirpy voice provides a degree of comfort.

We enter the very same claustrophobic room where Hans and the programmers treated me so poorly, but it has been transformed. Clean, tidy, with one large desk and several screens. A coffee machine. Rio checks I am comfortable, explaining how I am in her care all morning. If I need the toilet, or fresh air, she will accompany me. It is imperative, she says, that I am ready, in position, well before the appointed hour of eleven o'clock.

'Rio, I don't really understand what is going on,' I break my silence.

'Poppy, that's the whole point. You are the innocent child of Caernef, remember.'

'Wish I was at Caernef now. I have grown to hate Tarquin.'

'If all goes to plan, I will organise a runner to take you home to Caernef this afternoon.'

I feel a huge wave of relief. 'And if not?'

'There is a Plan B, a Plan C and a Plan D. However, I am confident that all will run smoothly.'

Rio flicks switches, attends to passwords and security encryption, before the screens all light up, all showing the same view. A headland, not Caernef, waves crashing against cliffs. A colony of gannets. Unspoilt. I sigh.

The drone camera pans along the shore, swinging slowly up on to the clifftop. Rough tussocky grass, ling. Then it zooms out, revealing …

'Oh.'

'I said that, the first time, too. It really hits you.'

'Yes,' I say, my eyes fixed on the launchpads, the rockets, the low glass buildings with sedum rooves and the azure sky behind them. 'Is it real, or virtuality?'

'It's real.'

'Oh.'

'While you have been sheltered at Higher Aynho, the eyes of the world have been on this beautiful headland. We couldn't have been blessed with better weather.'

I remember how disruptive it was when I was a child, and Robin became The Story. We had to have armed guards. The media wouldn't go away, until Miranda courageously intervened. That got her into a load of trouble. I bet the people who live on this once isolated and stunning headland have been as plagued as we were.

'Why, Rio?'

'It has been the biggest eco-conference ever. Robin gave an amazing speech last night. Guests from all over the world. And today the two rockets will take a selected few on the trip to the future. #YearZero is already trending.'

'But what about #FutureProof?'

'That too.'

…………

At half past ten, I am poised beside Rio. The digital pad is connected to Rio's computer. She has tested it is working a hundred times. The camera is ready to run. But I don't know which finger to use, on which hand.

She has set up one screen to show us virtuality. Apparently, Nathan is controlling that from Cyber City. It is as if I am inside the cybergame, a created character ready to play their part, watching for their cue.

The dignitaries are emerging from the glass buildings.

Rio recognises many of them. I don't take much interest in it. Perhaps I should.

'That's the Russian president, and the Chinese. Oh, and there is the Leader of Hezbollah.

'Why are all those leaders there. They don't support a peaceful, ecologically driven future? What's going on, Rio?'

'They are all on board.'

'What?'

We watch a tiny figure being helped on to a podium. It's Robin. Her words are reproduced instantly as text: *Friends, today is unprecedented. I must thank you all for your support, for sharing in our vision for the future of our sacred planet. We, of different faiths, different nationalities, even different fundamental beliefs, all come together to agree a shared plan to future proof the planet.*

Cheers, applause. The usual enthusiastic response to her motivational speeches, but from leaders of countries that have hitherto totally opposed zero carbon targets, anti-war treaties, indeed any real meaningful diplomatic cooperation at all. I know that much. This is either an incredible achievement, or some sort of trick.

Robin talks about her intention to inspire world leaders as signatories to a new plan, with targets to reverse the decline of many threatened species. She rounds up by hoping for brighter times ahead, with new generations being custodians of the planet. Delegates are cheered as they ascend a lift in the tall gantry, and one by one, enter the first capsule, waving, no doubt to the zillions of virtuality followers.

'What do I have to do, Rio. This all seems very important, but here it is just you and I in a funny little office under Tarquin.'

'At eleven o'clock, you will be asked to place your finger on the pad, there. It's simple really.'

In only twenty minutes.

We watch close-ups of the dignitaries belting up, each with their own window. Zoom into smiling faces, waving hands. An upbeat atmosphere. Now I can see the second capsule filling up. Less razmataz. 'Rio, there's Miranda!'

'Yes, but …'

'But what?'

'I thought she was going in the other rocket, the one with the … with the Year Zero brigade.'

'Oh.'

Rio is looking worried.

'Look, Robin is there too,' I observe.

'And Reginald De Vere.'

'Hm.'

Rio is frantically messaging Nathan. 'Nathan says it's all in hand. He has the keycode ready for virtuality.'

'Is it 49909-008 by any chance?'

'Poppy! How do you know that!'

'I pick up on things.'

'Suppose it's another randomly generated code, like all the others.' Rio mumbles.

'Not at all! It began when I was very young. Some … important guests visited Caernef. They played peek-a-boo with me on the veranda, and the code 49909-008 was devised. Read it backwards Rio, un-focus your eyes.'

'Boo Poppy!'

'That's me. Should have been 419-008,' I say.

'Hah! *Boo Pia!* I always said you were sharp,' she laughs. But this diversion isn't helpful as there seems to be some confusion on the platforms by the capsules. Virtuality blinks and suddenly goes offline.

'Shit.' Rio is tapping away to Nathan. She mutters, uneasily; 'He says it's okay. He says go ahead.'

Four minutes to eleven. 'Rio, I don't like rocket emissions. I don't like the rocket fuel. I don't like what they are doing to that beautiful habitat. This isn't what I thought it would be.'

'But Poppy, you wouldn't block this whole programme because of the emissions? #FutureProof is so much bigger than the rockets themselves. Surely you can see that?'

Two minutes to eleven. Do I do it? Which hand do I use. My left hand was the original template. My right hand is the replacement. Do I want to activate whatever this is, or to plead innocence and shove my left forefinger on the pad? Can I scupper the whole pageant?

Virtuality flickers back into view, showing Pia. Simultaneously, there I am, in the underground boardroom at Tarquin, placing my finger tentatively over the switch, poised. Two screens. Virtual and real. Everything seems normal. The booster engines fire up. There is no talk of aborting. I get ready.

The split second comes in great confusion. Rio nods. I place my left forefinger on the pad, and close my eyes.

Nothing happens.

'Press hard Poppy. It's not working.' Rio is urgent.

'They got my hand wrong.' I say calmly.

'What? Poppy!'

I raise my right hand ceremonially, and with a flourish, press my right forefinger on the pad, holding it in place.'

All at once, Pia reappears in virtuality, and I appear in the real-life feed. Together we are pressing our fingers firmly on to the digital trigger, me with my left hand and Pia using her right. Will anyone notice? Does it matter?'

'Has it worked this time Rio? I ask desperately, as the two booster rockets stand firm, flames and high-pressure gases bursting at the base. The capsules. Miranda, Robin, De Vere. The rockets blast off, simultaneously, with an immense roar. Birds flap in alarm. Tears prick my cheeks. I'm not sure, not at all sure. This is simply a ridiculous piece of cyber theatre. It's not going to help #FutureProof at all.

In reality, and in virtuality, the rockets soar through the azure sky, higher and higher, until they are just tiny dots on the screen. I can't watch any more, and cover my eyes.

'Can I go home now, Rio? Please?'

'Don't you want to watch the rockets re-engage, and the capsules come back down? It's so clever, these reusable boosters. The capsules will fall into the ocean. It's quite a show. It won't be that long; they are only up in the suborbital zone for twenty minutes or so. Tell you what, I'll make us a pot of tea. The coffee is foul. Then I will book you a car to take you home to Caernef in an hour or so. How does that sound?'

'Okay. Thanks Rio.' I say to please her.

While Rio fusses with the kettle and the teapot, just like Mum does, I watch the clip of Pia, which is on a loop, because we haven't entered the game, and try to lose myself in the deceptively gentle melody. Violins. A flute. No doubt Cai, Rick, along with the hordes of virtuality addicts are swiping and tapping, enjoying their ride in Future Galactic, paying their sponsorship to virtuality, which Nathan will pass on to #FutureProof. It's all a game to them, to Nathan, to Cai, to Rick, to Miranda. But life isn't a game. Robin knows that. My new friends in Higher Aynho know that. I'm relieved not to be playing it myself, or watching over Cai's shoulder.

We drink three cups of tea. The capsules don't come down.

....

By half-past four, the sun has set on this bizarre day. Rio and I watched one capsule descend dramatically into the sea, slowed by parachutes, just as intended. But the second never came down. There was no explosion, no tracking by satellite or radar. It's like it disappeared into a black hole. The rocket with Miranda, Robin and De Vere on board, as well as the Chinese, Russian and other dubious leaders. People are talking of terrorism, of an accident. But, as yet, there is no evidence of anything.

Totally deflated, and exhausted, I have pleaded with Rio to go home. She is frantically busy messaging, and trying to locate the rocket. I bid her farewell and head for the grandiose conservatory, to await my transport.

My phone rings. I had almost forgotten what it's like having one. It's Rick.

'Poppy, get out of Tarquin NOW. Get out; anywhere. You are in danger. Go now. Tell me you're going.'

'But what about Rio? The staff. Everyone else here?'

'Poppy, I am only concerned with you. Don't delay. Just get out! Now! I got into Miranda's phone, I worked on it all night. There was a link to a cyberhacker. I picked up all sorts. They are after Miranda, and that De Vere bloke. They are after *you*, and they know you are at Tarquin. Now GET OUT!'

I run to reception, batter the fire alarm with a metal chair, aiming the leg straight at the glass membrane. Bells. People. Chaos. I run. I run down the drive, putting as much distance between me and the ancient building as I can.

A massive blast; Tarquin appears to explode. Fireballs. Hit after hit.

I should help, but I am a heap of jelly. An ecocar draws up. The runner driving it calls to me, 'Poppy? Poppy Kiwan? I'd know you anywhere. Pia of course. What the hell is going on here?'

She bundles me into the passenger seat and accelerates away from the maelstrom. I try to speak, but am totally incoherent.

'I've been instructed to take you home to Caernef. Just try to relax.'

I sit, totally numb, throughout the interminable journey, not daring to even get out my phone.

17: ARCADIAN B

At midnight, I scramble out of the ecocar by the gate to Caernef, thanking the runner, and sprinting home. Don't even pause to listen for owls. My feet find their way through the night, but home is darkness. I bang on the door. No one is in. Mum and Dad are *always* here. This isn't right. Without a door key, I try the downstairs windows, but all are shut tight.

With sore chill fingers, I give up, for now, and run down the path to the arcade, retrieve my hidden key with no difficulty, open up, and close the door firmly behind me. By the light of the moon, I sit on my stool. Breathe. Long and slow. At least I'm home. I'm safe. Must contact Rick in the morning.

Lock the arcade and run over the clifftop towards the folly, expecting it to be unoccupied. With tears in my eyes, I stop and stare up at Robin's vacant window, in darkness. I fumble under the stones to locate her hidden key, and gain entry.

The folly smells of herbs and tea. My feet echo as I pound up the stairs and perch on Robin's chair, where I pause, gazing out at the moonlit estuary, like she has done so many times. I have been truly blessed to grow up here, but I could have done without all the intrigue and espionage. It taints the wildness. I am thinking that you cannot achieve equity and protect the natural world without politics. I notice the wooden box on Robin's bed.

She must have been looking at it before she left. Left for the last time.

I have watched her slide the secret compartment open so many times. The key drops out, and I manoeuvre the wooden panel to reveal the keyhole, turn the key, and take out the two cigarette boxes that Gid gave me, now rather squashed, after ten years of handling. The contents, however, are the same as on the day I chose them for Robin. I was an adoring and innocent young child. She had just returned from stopping the glitch. With reverence, I stroke the bright blue jay's feather, the empty snail shells, lichen and acorns. I inhale the faint scent of the dried flowers, snippets of herbs, and there is the fragment of paper, with my childish scrawl, *from Poppy xxx*. With tears pricking the back of my eyes, I remove my whin necklace, and add it to Robin's treasures in her wooden box. She is gone. Gone forever. I had not realised how much I depended upon Robin to always be there, for me, for the world. Robin's runners, the earths.

Lights approaching down the path. I left the door unlocked. Didn't expect anyone at this hour, with Robin … gone.

Voices downstairs. *You left it unlocked Robin! You'll be okay? See you in the morning then. If you're sure.*

They leave. I hurry down, coming face to face with … Robin at the foot of the stairs. We fall into each other's arms.

'Oh Poppy, your parents, and Cai, will be so pleased to see you when they come back tomorrow.'

'Robin, I thought you were …'

'You didn't think I would go with them, did you Poppy? No, my dear. I am needed here; we have the runners, the earths need our support, and, of course, there is my #FutureProof to deliver. I slipped out at the last minute, and watched them leave, from the top of the gantry. Not really permitted, but well … She knew what she was doing, Miranda. They trusted her, you see. If she was on board, with Reginald, they believed they would come back, but …'

'Miranda is …'

'She is up there in the cosmos. The ultimate hero if ever there was one. Martyr, I suppose.'

'How?'

'I don't understand how they did it. The science is beyond me. But I do understand that Miranda's final act was totally selfless. She gave her life for the world to be rid of those … those … Oh yes, as I left, Miranda gave me this. Her final words, as I rushed out, were *give it to Poppy*. Miranda was never one for great long speeches, and time was limited, but here you are.'

Robin hands me Arcadian B.

I help her up the stairs, place Arcadian B in her box, then head to the kitchen to make us both a cup of tea.

The End

Other Books By Chris Malone:

In #stoptheglitch, narrated by Robin, catastrophic failure of world systems, notably the internet, throws society into complete disarray. Robin and her friends establish an eco community and education centre, Caernef Camp, on a remote Welsh clifftop. They are drawn into attempts to stop the cyberterrorism believed to be behind the *glitch*.

#isolate picks up the story from Miranda's perspective, exploring the tensions between Robin and Miranda. From her clifftop folly, Robin leads a successful plot to influence the outcome of the 2024 general election through mobilising alternative communities, *earths*, connected by *runners*.

Poppy is a toddler in #stoptheglitch, a child in #isolate, and then a teenager, who narrates #FutureProof. She has lived off-grid at Caernef Camp throughout her life, and feels alienated by the dominance of digital existence in the 2030s. Poppy cannot escape the espionage surrounding her unusual upbringing. She has a key part to play in the #FutureProof project, uniting reality with the virtual world, to rid the earth of evil despots.

CHRIS MALONE
A SCHOOL INSPECTOR CALLS
But who is the fool in the school?

ABOUT THE AUTHOR

After retiring from a busy education career, Chris was the first female thriller author to join Burton Mayers Books. Following the successful publication of *#stoptheglitch* and *#isolate*, *#FutureProof* now completes the trilogy. Chris also worked with Burton Mayers Books on the publication of *A School Inspector Calls, but who is the fool in the school.*

Having returned, with her husband, to live in Herefordshire, Chris is now enjoying a quieter pace of life, renovating the house, rewilding the garden, reading, writing and campaigning. She has willingly swapped her smart black heels for sturdy boots.

Milton Keynes UK
Ingram Content Group UK Ltd.
UKHW040726161023
430697UK00005B/219